THE MYSTERY OF THE HAUNTED CAVES

Penny Warner

Meadowbrook Press

Distributed by Simon & Schuster
New York

Library of Congress Cataloging-in-Publication Data

Warner, Penny.
    The mystery of the haunted caves/Penny Warner.
       p. cm. -- (Troop 13 mysteries)
    Summary: Four friends search for treasure during a scout outing to
California gold rush country.
    Publisher's ISBN 0-88166-390-5
    Simon & Schuster ordering #0-689-84562-6
    [1. Girl Scouts--Fiction. 2. Camping--Fiction. 3. Caving--Fiction. 4.
Buried treasure--Fiction. 5. California--Fiction] I. Title.

PZ7.W2458 My 2001
[Fic]--dc21   00-068376

Managing Editor: Christine Zuchora-Walske
Editor: Megan McGinnis
Proofreader: Angela Wiechmann
Production Manager: Paul Woods
Cover Illustrator: Paul Casale

© 2001 by Penny Warner

Published by: Meadowbrook Press
                 5451 Smetana Drive, Minnetonka, MN 55343

                 www.meadowbrookpress.com

BOOK TRADE DISTRIBUTION by Simon & Schuster, a division of Simon
and Schuster, Inc., 1230 Avenue of the Americas, New York, NY 10020

05 04 03 02 01   12 11 10 9 8 7 6 5 4 3 2 1

Printed in the United States of America

Dedication

To Tom, Matthew, and Rebecca
and
to Girl Scouts everywhere.

Acknowledgments

Many thanks to all those who contributed to the story: Susan Anderson, Donna Andrews, Taffy Cannon, Colleen Casey, Helen Chappell, AvaDianne Day, Karen Dyer, Jerrilyn Farmer, Sally Fellows, Margery Flax, Anne Grant, Maryelizabeth Hart, Ann Hilgeman, Mary Keenan, Rena Leith, Kristin Littlefield, Maria Lima, Carol McCoy, Shirley McDermott, Doris Ann Norris, Ann Parker, Jo Peters, Connie Pike, Diane Plumley, Barbara Rosengarten, Susan Rust, Shannon Stoeckinger, Kathleen Taylor, Pam Thomson, Kathy Vaughn, Susan Warner, Jennifer Wendel, Dina Willner, and all the Teabuds.

A special thanks to my wonderful publisher, Bruce Lansky, and my terrific editors, Megan McGinnis and Christine Zuchora-Walske.

Chapter 1

"If we don't beat Troop 7 this year, I'm going to...to eat a bat sandwich!" thirteen-year-old Becca Matthews announced to her three best friends as she stepped from the bus at Camp Miwok.

"How about a bat s'more?" CJ Tran planted her small feet in the red dirt of the California Gold Country. "Bats taste better with chocolate."

Becca laughed. It'd been a long, winding, three-hour drive from San Francisco to Camp Miwok for the scouts' Gold Rush Jamboree. The last hour had been especially bumpy. Luckily, CJ's jokes had entertained all eight members of Troop 13—and helped keep Becca from getting bus sick.

Becca pulled her long blond hair back into a ponytail and wiped the sweat from her neck. "It's a whole lot hotter here than in the city," she thought. It looked a whole lot different, too. The jagged lava rocks scattered about made the terrain look moonlike. She took a deep breath of country air—and crinkled her nose. Skunk.

"I wonder what it was like living here back when the Gold Rush began," she said, remembering the sleepy little town they'd just driven through, with its lack of movie theaters, pizza parlors, and music stores. "I heard the streets were 'paved with gold.'"

"Must have been a zoo with all those prospectors coming to

strike it rich," CJ said, stuffing a crossword puzzle into her back-pack. "I saw a couple of scruffy old men when we drove through town who looked like they've been here since 1849." She'd worked on the puzzle the whole bus ride. Becca wondered how she kept from getting bus sick.

"I've heard rumors there's still gold up here," Becca mused.

"I doubt it," Sierra Garcia said. She brushed her thick brown braid off her shoulder and slipped on her vest loaded with colorful badges. Becca envied her Outdoor Adventure badge and hoped to earn one herself this weekend. She had already made several campfire meals, gone on three hikes, packed a first-aid kit, and used a square knot in four different ways. All she had left to do to earn the badge was build a camp-fire and leave the site without a trace of use.

"You know, just 'cause you got that Geology Discovery badge last year doesn't mean you know whether there's gold up here." Becca playfully threw a pine cone at her friend. Except Sierra probably *did* know. She was crazy about rocks, minerals, and anything else that had to do with nature. She even knew the difference between a stalagmite and stalactite. Becca could never remember which one went up and which one went down.

"Actually," Sierra continued, "the so-called gold country is mostly just ghost towns and empty mines now. The brochure I have says there are still some descendants of the original miners living here, but most of them just try to mine money out of the tourists."

"What about the story of Black Bart's hidden treasure?" Becca reminded them. According to stories she'd read, after Black Bart robbed prospectors of their gold, he hid the treasure in the Haunted Caves. When he disappeared, no one ever found it.

"And don't forget the Haunted Caves," Jonnie Jackson added, echoing Becca's thoughts. "After all, they're one of the reasons we're here. You know why people think they're haunted, don't you?"

"Yeah, they moan...for the same reason we do: CJ's jokes!" Becca said.

CJ pretended to look offended.

Jonnie laughed. "Well, we better not be moaning tomorrow. I want to be cheering—after we win! We came so close to winning the gold medal last year," she said, twisting one of her tight black braids. Becca noticed Jonnie always did that whenever she was nervous or upset. "We've *got* to win this time. We've been preparing all year."

Becca could almost feel the cool gold medal against her skin. The Jamboree comprised four events: rappelling (climbing down a steep cliff using a rope); spelunking (finding your way through a cave); puzzle solving (figuring out answers to puzzling questions); and nonviolent animal trapping (catching an animal without harming it).

The first event was all up to Jonnie, the best athlete in Troop 13. She loved to hike and climb, and Becca was certain she'd win the rappelling event.

"Don't worry. We'll beat Troop 7," replied CJ optimistically, as she unloaded her gear from the bus's storage compartment.

"I hope you're right, CJ," answered Jonnie. "After what they did to us when they won last year, putting all those ants in our clothes... I couldn't stand to see Troop 7 win again."

CJ shuddered at the memory. "Well, this year we've all been training hard for our events. I studied the puzzle solving clues from last year's Jamboree, and I'm pretty sure I can crack this year's puzzles," she said.

"Sure you can, CJ." Becca glanced over at the other troops. The competition looked tough, especially fourteen-year-old Tiffany Hewitt, the oldest girl in Troop 7.

Becca continued, "Sierra, I'm glad you're in charge of the spelunking event again, since you've got the best sense of direction."

Sierra nodded. "CJ, don't forget your flashlight this time," she teased. "It's pitch black in those caves."

CJ rolled her eyes.

"And Jonnie, you're so buff this year, you won't have any trouble rappelling into that cavern. That'll give us a great head start." Becca pulled her sleeping bag from the bus compartment and set it on the dusty ground.

Jonnie shrugged. "I just hope those ropes hold."

"Listen, my event is the only one we need to worry about." Becca gazed at the tall pines that bordered the camp. Sierra, CJ, and Jonnie gathered around her as the rest of Troop 13 headed for the campsite.

"Look, Becca," Sierra said. "It wasn't your fault we lost the Jamboree last year. That was a great animal trap you designed."

"Yeah, right." Frowning, Becca sat on one of the large lava rocks and unzipped her backpack. She pulled out her laptop and checked it for damage. "If you remember, that's the one event we lost big time. Thanks to me."

"Hey, girlfriend," Jonnie sat beside Becca. "That trap was so cool! It wasn't your fault you trapped the wrong animal."

"Yeah, Becca. It isn't easy to tell a real bear from old Mrs. Stumplemeyer!" CJ added.

Sierra and Jonnie giggled.

Becca grinned. "I didn't mean for her to get caught, I swear!"

All four girls howled at the memory of Troop 7's leader accidentally tumbling into Troop 13's trap and landing on her rear end.

"I totally cracked up!" Jonnie wiped her eyes. "I don't think Troop 7 ever got over that."

Becca laughed so hard she snorted, which made the girls laugh even more. Calming down, she said, "Well, I'm determined to win the gold medal this year. I've found instructions on this web site for a trap that's even better—"

"Scouts!"

It was Susan Sanford calling from their campsite. She'd been Troop 13's leader for two years. The girls admired her leadership skills, sense of humor, and warm smile, not to mention her tall, athletic build and gorgeous brown hair. Becca was grateful her troop didn't have Mrs. Stumplemeyer for its leader. Susan really seemed to enjoy coming up with fun adventures. All Mrs. Stumplemeyer seemed to enjoy doing was giving orders to her scouts while glaring at the other troops.

"Becca, CJ, Sierra, Jonnie, Courtney, Kelly, Jennifer, and Melissa," Susan held up two fingers, the sign for quiet. Troop 13 hushed.

"Uh-oh," Becca muttered. "Time to get to work."

"It's time to get to work!"

Susan's words set the girls in motion. Camp Miwok bustled with activity as the scouts pitched their tents, stored their gear, and lit their campfires. Troop 13 pitched two tents, one for Becca, CJ, Sierra, and Jonnie and one for the other four girls. Susan had a tent to herself. Two hours later, the camp looked like a tent village nestled among the pines.

The troops first enjoyed a dinner of pigs in a blanket and s'mores (batless), then sang campfire songs and told ghost stories around the burning logs. When the sun set and the stars came out, it was time to hit the sleeping bags.

After saying good-night to their troopmates and Susan, the four friends spent the few minutes before lights out working on projects. Sierra flipped through her guidebooks on caves. Jonnie and CJ practiced fingerspelling and sign language for the Community Care badges they were earning. Becca turned on her laptop and wireless modem.

"There's an e-mail here from your mom, Sierra," Becca said. "Want me to read it to you?"

"Sure. But she's probably just going to tell me to brush my teeth, watch out for poison oak, and stay away from the boys' camp."

CJ giggled. "Well, if there are any boys up here, we'll find them, so *that's* not going to happen!"

Sierra threw a pillow at her, and a pillow fight broke out. Becca joined in but quickly returned to her laptop.

"Okay, Sierra, do you want to hear this message or not?" She was eager to get onto the Internet and search for cave maps.

"Sure." Sierra swatted Jonnie's head with a pillow one last time.

"'Dear Sierra: I hope you and Becca and Jonnie and CJ and the rest of the troop are having a good time. Have fun, do your best, don't forget to brush your teeth, and watch out for poison oak!'"

"At least we don't have to stay away from boys," Sierra said.

"What boys? There are no boys around here! It's all girls!"

The girls burst into giggles and collapsed on their sleeping bags.

"I can't wait for tomorrow," Jonnie sighed, pulling her teddy bear from her backpack. Becca knew she never went anywhere without Brownie the Bear. "I probably won't be able to sleep tonight!"

"Oh yes, you will," said Sierra. "When CJ starts going on about how she solved her latest puzzle, we'll all be totally bored to sleep!"

"Hey, I'll do what I can to help our star athlete," CJ shot back, smiling at Jonnie.

"Flashlights out!" Susan called. One by one, the tents grew dark. Within minutes, Becca's tentmates were asleep.

But not Becca. She lay in her sleeping bag, staring at her laptop screen. It wasn't worrying about tomorrow's events that was keeping her awake, but something she'd found on the Web, which had nothing to do with the plentiful spiders crawling all over Camp Miwok. She'd done some virtual digging into the Haunted Caves, hoping to find information that might give her troop an edge in tomorrow's events, and had found maps, history, bat sightings, geological formations…and something else: the legend of Black Bart and his hidden gold.

"Wouldn't it be so cool," Becca thought, her heart racing as she shut down the laptop, "if we just happened to find it!"

After tossing and turning for what seemed like hours, Becca gave up trying to fall asleep. There was only one way to deal with this excess energy. She switched on her flashlight and rummaged through her backpack.

"CJ! Jonnie! Sierra! Wake up!" she whispered.

The girls moaned and rolled over.

"Why'd you wake us up?" CJ complained. "I was dreaming I was in a boy band!"

"What is it? Lions? Tigers? Bears? Mrs. Stumplemeyer?" Jonnie rubbed her eyes.

"Do you know what time it is?" Sierra yawned and checked her glow-in-the-dark watch.

Becca nodded. "Yeah, it's payback time." With one hand she held up a plastic sandwich bag full of safety pins. With the other hand she held a red marker.

CJ blinked. "What's that stuff for?"

Becca grinned.

Sierra and Jonnie caught on immediately and tossed back their covers.

"Oh, cool!" CJ giggled as she scrambled after her friends, who were already creeping outside. The girls tiptoed among the tents in the moonlight. The smell of skunk pierced the air. Only an occasional distant howl broke the stillness.

And while Tiffany and her tentmates dreamed about winning the gold medal, the four girls from Troop 13 stood just outside the tent, unfastening the safety pins and uncapping the red marker...

Chapter 2

"He-e-elp!"

"Get us out of here!"

"Something's after us!"

"We're trapped!"

Screams from one of Troop 7's tents woke the entire camp at dawn. Girls in pajamas, nighties, and long T-shirts scrambled out of their tents to see what was up.

Becca, CJ, Jonnie, and Sierra stayed put in their tent, peeking out as everyone else gathered around Tiffany's tent. Even from a distance, they could see the tent shaking as Tiffany and her friends tried to escape.

Through her binoculars Becca admired the red bull's-eye and message on the tent: "Hit the bull's-eye and win a prize!" Several girls were bombarding the target with pine cones that had been stacked conveniently nearby. Becca aimed the binoculars at the tent's door. Safety pins immobilized the three zippers. It took several minutes for the shower of pine cones and the laughter to subside so someone could undo the pins and free the four girls. Tiffany, Gina, Joanne, and Stephanie ran for the latrine.

"I guess they really had to go!" said Becca, grinning.

"Badly!" CJ agreed.

Soon after, they heard Tiffany yelling, "Those dorks from

Troop 13 did this!"

"How does she know it's us?" CJ whispered. Then she realized they'd been the only ones who hadn't come out to watch the fun.

Jonnie peered out the door flap. "Uh-oh," she said, "here they come."

Four girls from Troop 7 were stalking over. Tiffany led the way, wearing silky pink pajamas and fluffy slippers. A sweatshirt was tied around her waist.

Becca stepped out of the tent in her holey "Girls Rule!" T-shirt and sweatpants, staring at Tiffany. "What happened?" she asked. "We heard all the screaming—"

Tiffany cut Becca off. "*You* did that! You and your stupid little pals! Those dumb pine cones woke us up…and we couldn't get out to use the—to see what was going on!"

"Wow, that's awful!" Becca said innocently.

Tiffany tightened the sweatshirt around her waist. "You nimrod. We know you were behind it. That prank was just the sort of dorky thing you would do. What if we had an acci—emergency? You know the rules: Any scout who doesn't respect others is not a good scout! Trapping us in our tents is disrespectful!"

Becca tried not to laugh. "You mean like putting ants in people's clothes?"

Tiffany clenched her fists and stepped forward menacingly.

"Girls!" Susan suddenly called out. "Time to make breakfast!"

Tiffany glared at the girls from Troop 13. "We'll get you for this," she hissed. "We're gonna kick your butts at the rappelling competition, just like we did last year!"

As Tiffany stomped off, Becca stared at her sweatshirt. Was that a wet spot?

"Girls! Breakfast!" Susan repeated, eyeing them suspiciously. The four friends stifled their giggles and hustled to dress.

A half-hour later, the scouts were dressed in jeans or khaki shorts and T-shirts. Some wore their badge-covered vests.

Breakfast consisted of muffin cup bacon 'n' eggs, biscuits in a can, orange juice, and hot cocoa. Each troop prepared its own meal, the scouts taking turns lighting the campfire, cooking the food, and cleaning up. As the girls from Troop 13 wolfed down their breakfast, they discussed the first event of the day: rappelling.

"Onnie's gah dish dow," Sierra said, her mouth full of biscuit. She watched Jonnie check her rappelling equipment. Swallowing, she continued, "It'll be easy for her."

Becca agreed. Jonnie was strong and fast, and she'd done lots of mountain climbing. She'd have no trouble rappelling into the hundred-foot cavern. But would she beat Tiffany, Troop 7's rappeller?

"Remember, she's got to get down there fast," CJ said, "but not so fast she loses control of her ropes and harness."

The three girls shuddered at the horrific thought.

"Did you hear about that new scout?" Sierra asked, changing the subject.

Becca shook her head. "Who?"

"Amber something, from Troop 10. She's supposed to be some kind of super-athlete. She's been bragging about being a real rock climber, not just a gym rat." Sierra pointed out Amber at Troop 10's campsite.

Becca glanced over at the new girl and sized her up. Amber was tall and lanky like Jonnie, with tight black curls covered with butterfly clips. It was hard to tell how strong she was under her baggy clothes, but it looked as if Tiffany wasn't the only one Jonnie would have to beat.

"Time to go!" Susan announced. The troops hiked up the dirt road to the Haunted Caves in less than a half-hour. Inside the caves, the park rangers and troop leaders checked the harnesses, ropes, buckles, and helmets, making sure every piece of equipment was safe.

Becca glanced over the cavern's edge. The steep cliff dropped away into a seemingly bottomless pit. She saw nothing but blackness below and shivered, thankful this was Jonnie's event.

"All right, girls," boomed Mrs. Stumplemeyer, Troop 7's leader. "You know the rules, but I'm going to review them." The girls groaned. Mrs. Stumplemeyer held up two fingers, but it was her stern look that silenced them.

"When I give the command," Mrs. Stumplemeyer explained, "use your ropes to lower yourselves to the bottom of the cavern within the allotted time. If you're too slow or too fast, you'll be disqualified. We want you to rappel responsibly, not barrel down out of control. The first scout to make it to the bottom *within the time window* wins this event. We'll be down there waiting for you."

Jonnie nervously checked her watch, then stretched her muscles for the zillionth time. Becca could tell she was anxious to start. A lot depended on her winning the first event.

"Hang in there," CJ said, laughing at her pun. "Get it? See you at the bottom."

"One way or another," Jonnie replied with a tight smile.

The girls gave Jonnie a few more encouraging words before descending a spiral staircase to the cavern floor, where they'd greet the rappellers with cheers and hugs as they landed.

"Climbing down these stairs must be almost as nerve-racking as rappelling," Becca thought, as the metal structure shook. At the bottom, the damp, cold air chilled her, and she slipped on the sweatshirt tied around her waist. Gazing up, she imagined the Statue of Liberty could fit in the huge space.

Becca lifted her binoculars and spotted Jonnie between Tiffany and Amber. She waved her flashlight to signal her support. A hush fell over the crowd as the tiny figures above switched on their helmet lights.

Tweeeet! Mrs. Stumplemeyer's whistle echoed in the cavern.

The ten rappellers began their descent, guided only by their troopmates' dim flashlights.

"What's happening?" Sierra asked Becca, who was still peering through the binoculars.

"Jonnie's way ahead of everyone." Becca paused. "But that new girl—Amber—she's picking up speed."

Becca shared her binoculars with Sierra and CJ as the rappellers completed the first fifty feet of the descent, creeping down the cliff on their ropes like spiders trailing silk.

Becca took the binoculars from Sierra and focused them on Jonnie. Suddenly she gasped. "Oh no! Amber just passed Jonnie!" Becca's heart thumped. She searched for Tiffany and found her a few feet above Jonnie.

The other girls didn't need binoculars to see what had

happened. Amber had taken the lead. No one from Troop 13 said anything, but the girls from Troop 10 began to chant, "*Am*-ber! *Am*-ber! *Am*—"

Suddenly the chanting stopped. The scouts' murmuring indicated something was wrong. Amber had stopped her descent. Through her binoculars, Becca saw it all up close.

"Oh my gosh! Amber's stuck! She seems to be floating in midair."

Sierra snatched the binoculars and studied Amber. "She's wiggling around…her rope must be caught on something."

Becca took back the binoculars and zeroed in on Jonnie, who had almost caught up with Amber. Tiffany was right behind Jonnie. The other rappellers had stopped descending to watch Amber squirming frantically, suspended in space.

Becca focused on Amber. "She's definitely caught on something; it looks like a rough ledge sticking out of the cliff. Her rope…" Becca paused, straining to make out what Amber was doing. "She's trying to get free…but every time she wiggles around, the rope rubs against that ledge and…oh no…"

"What?" CJ shouted.

"The rope…it's…fraying!"

A hush fell over the crowd as everyone realized the danger Amber was in. The sharp edge of the jutting ledge was sawing away at her lifeline.

Becca aimed the binoculars at Jonnie again. "Uh-oh."

"What now?" CJ grabbed at the binoculars, but Becca jerked out of reach.

"Something's wrong with Jonnie now. She's slowing

down," Becca said.

"Why?" Sierra asked. "Is she stuck, too?"

"I can't tell, but she's definitely stopped." Becca gasped. "She's...trying to reach Amber!"

The three girls looked at one another. "But what about the contest?" CJ said. "Tiffany's almost caught up with her!"

If Jonnie continued her descent now, she would win the rappelling event. But instead she began swinging her legs back and forth.

Becca saw Tiffany pause for a moment when she reached Jonnie and Amber. Jonnie, still swinging her legs, yelled to Tiffany, but Becca couldn't hear the words over the spectators' concerned chatter. Tiffany didn't seem to hear Jonnie either. Or she'd chosen to ignore her. She slid past Jonnie and Amber, continuing her descent.

Tiffany had taken the lead.

The girls from Troop 7 began to cheer louder and louder as their troopmate rappelled toward the bottom of the cavern and victory. Becca kept her eyes on Jonnie, who continued swinging her legs, trying to reach Amber. Amber looked terrified as she squirmed around, trying to free herself.

"Oh no!" Becca whispered.

"What?" CJ squealed.

"The rope...another strand is about to—"

The strand broke before Becca could finish her sentence. Amber jerked downward a foot. She screamed, and so did the girls at the bottom of the cavern.

Becca focused on Jonnie. "Come on, Jonnie, come on," she

murmured. Jonnie swung her legs for several more seconds, try-ing to gain momentum. She was only two feet from reaching Amber. Becca could see the girl crying as she reached out for Jonnie.

With one more vigorous kick, Jonnie finally was able to grab Amber's outstretched arm. Amber threw her arms around Jonnie like a lost toddler who'd just found her mother.

Gripping Amber with one hand, Jonnie found a foothold on the cliff and struggled out of her sweatshirt. She wrapped it around Amber's waist and her own, tying the sleeves tightly with a knot she'd learned for her camping badge. Then Jonnie opened her fanny pack and pulled out her metal flashlight. She lifted it and slammed it against the sharp, thin edge of the ledge. Becca watched the rocky tip break off and fall to the ground.

Amber jerked as her rope was freed, but she clung to Jonnie, and the sweatshirt held them tightly together. With one strong rope and one frayed nearly in half, the two girls slowly started to descend.

"She's free!" A cheer erupted from the cavern floor. The girls hugged each other, while the leaders wiped sweat from their fore-heads. Everyone was happy to see that Amber was out of danger. Soon the girls were only five or six feet from landing.

And then Amber's rope snapped. Jonnie's rope couldn't handle the jolt of extra weight, and the girls plummeted the last few feet.

The two landed hard enough to knock the wind out of them. As they gasped and coughed, their troopmates gathered around and helped them to their feet. It was clear from the cheers that both Amber and Jonnie were going to be all right.

But the members of Troop 7 were cheering for a different reason. Tiffany had landed several minutes before Amber and Jonnie. Troop 7 had won the rappelling event.

Chapter 3

"Losers!" Tiffany sneered at Troop 13. "I told you we were going to beat you this year!"

Becca shook her head, then turned to help Jonnie remove her gear. Jonnie didn't look so good. "Are you all right?" Becca asked as she unhooked one of Jonnie's ropes. "You were amazing!"

"But we lost the event," Jonnie protested, "thanks to me."

"Jonnie!" CJ said. "You did the right thing. You saved Amber's life. And you risked your life to do it!"

Sierra chimed in. "I thought what you did was great. So what if we didn't win? That's not the point."

"The girls are right, Jonnie," came a voice from the darkness. Susan stepped forward, holding her flashlight. "You're a scout, and that means you help others when they're in trouble. I'm very proud of you." She put her arm around Jonnie and gave her a squeeze. Jonnie's look of disappointment faded a little.

Becca glanced over at Tiffany, who was accepting congratulations from her circle of friends. "I just wish Troop 7 hadn't won. They're driving us nuts with all their bragging."

"Scouts! Sco-o-u-uts!" Mrs. Stumplemeyer's voice echoed like a siren. The girls quieted down, hoping she wouldn't blow her whistle again. Mrs. Stumplemeyer's voice was shrill enough.

"We have our winner of the first event! I'm pleased to

announce that thanks to Tiffany Hewitt, Troop 7 has won the rappelling event."

A spurt of applause followed—mostly from Troop 7.

"Yes, Mrs. Stumplemeyer," said Mrs. Parker, the leader of Troop 10—Amber's troop. She stepped forward, followed by several other troop leaders. "Troop 7 won the event. But we have another award to present."

"What do you mean, another award?" snapped Mrs. Stumplemeyer. "There's only one winner for the rappelling event. I don't see—"

Mrs. Parker interrupted, "It's great to be a winner, but it's even better to be a good scout—"

"What do you mean?" Mrs. Stumplemeyer broke in. "My girls are good scouts."

"Mrs. Stumplemeyer, you didn't let me finish," Mrs. Parker continued. "I was about to say that Amber was in serious danger up there, and a scout from another troop forfeited the race to rescue her. This is a stellar demonstration of the Scout Oath, 'To help others at all times.'"

"So?" said Mrs. Stumplemeyer, puzzled.

"So, while your scout has won the rappelling event," Mrs. Parker continued, "the other troop leaders and I believe that Jonnie Jackson from Troop 13 deserves an even higher honor— one of the highest honors a scout can receive: the Leadership Pin. She clearly gave up her winning edge to help Amber, and she has set a fine example for everyone."

"Yes, but—"

"This type of behavior should be rewarded, not punished.

Don't you agree, Mrs. Stumplemeyer?"

Troop 7's leader glanced at her scouts, then nodded weakly.

"Shall we take a vote?" asked Mrs. Parker. "All in favor that Jonnie Jackson from Troop 13 be awarded the Leadership Pin, raise your hands." Ninety percent of the hands went up. "Those opposed?" Several hands from Troop 7 started to go up, then faltered. Only one hand stayed up: Tiffany's.

Tiffany looked around with disgust. "It's not fair!" she whined. "You're just trying to downplay my award by giving her a better one! What about that prank they pulled on us this morning? *That* wasn't setting a good example!"

Susan stepped forward and stood face to face with Tiffany. "My girls didn't complain when you put their clothes on an anthill last year."

Tiffany muttered and stomped off.

A crowd gathered around Jonnie and congratulated her. Becca stood back and smiled at Susan. Susan winked and smiled back. It looked as if one good deed led to another. Troop 7 may have won the first event, but Troop 13 had won an even higher honor by doing the right thing.

Becca glanced over at the girls in Troop 7, who were huddled tightly and whispering.

"I wonder what they're up to," Sierra said to Becca.

"I don't know," Becca replied, "but I think we'd better zip up our tents tight tonight!"

Chapter 4

"I'm up next," Sierra said when the scouts returned to the caves after lunch. "But I have a feeling this event isn't going to be so easy. Not with Troop 7 wanting revenge." She zipped up her coveralls. "I'm ready, though."

"You go, girl!" CJ said, adjusting her helmet. She stepped inside the cave entrance and flicked on her headlight. The beam bounced off the walls as she surveyed the rocky room.

"Sierra, just get us in and get us out, that's all I ask," Becca said. She didn't like being in small spaces, especially small dark spaces. And spelunking meant she'd be crawling through lots of small dark spaces.

"Don't worry," Jonnie said. "Sierra has built-in radar."

"So do I," said CJ, her voice echoing in the cave. When she turned and saw the three girls' surprised faces, she grinned. "I can find a cute boy anywhere within fifty feet!"

Giggling, they finished putting on their gear.

Soon the troop leaders came by and gave each troop a map of the caves.

Sierra quickly studied the map. "Hey, this looks more like the puzzle solving event than the spelunking event," she said, pointing to the questions written next to each cave. Before the others could take a closer look, they heard…

"Giiirrlllss!" It was Mrs. Stumplemeyer again. She blew her whistle, and the scouts covered their ears—too late.

"I wish she wouldn't do that!" Becca wondered if everyone else's ears were ringing, too.

"Girls, your attention please," Mrs. Stumplemeyer commanded. "We're doing something new this year. As you can see on your maps, we're combining the spelunking and puzzle solving events. You must find your way through the caves and answer the questions on your maps. There will be rangers stationed throughout the caves in case you get into trouble, but if you call for assistance, your troop will be disqualified. Does everyone understand, or shall I go over it again?"

"No, we understand, Mrs. Stumplemeyer. Please don't go over it again," the scouts said flatly.

Sierra looked at CJ. "You're going to have to help me with this. I can handle the cave maneuvers, but you're the expert puzzle solver. You should stay up front with me."

CJ nodded and read over the questions on the map. Becca could see from CJ's anxious expression that they were going to be tough to answer.

"All right, troops, line up," Mrs. Stumplemeyer said. "We'll begin with Troop 3, followed by the remaining troops in numerical order at five-minute intervals. Remember, you only have one hour to get through the caves, write down your answers, and find your way out. The troop that correctly answers the most questions in the shortest amount of time wins the event. Any questions?"

"Yeah," Becca whispered. "Where's the emergency exit?"

Becca heard giggling. She turned and saw the girls from Troop 7.

"Scared?" Tiffany sneered.

Becca glared at her.

"You know about the legend, don't you?" Tiffany teased.

For a moment, Becca thought Tiffany meant the legend of Black Bart's treasure. "No," she hedged.

"These are called the Haunted Caves for a reason. Know why?"

Becca shrugged.

"Someone got lost in them a few years ago. A girl about your age—twelve."

"I'm thirteen."

"Whatever. Anyway, she was trying to find some lost gold, and no one ever saw her again. But they say you can hear her moan."

Becca blinked then swallowed. "Yeah, right," she squeaked.

Tiffany moaned long and low.

Becca shivered in spite of herself. She hoped no one saw. "Well, I'm not scared," she insisted. "I only wanted to know if there was an exit in case you start moaning for your mommy."

Tiffany flipped her long blond ponytail as she turned back to her friends. She whispered something to them, and they laughed again.

Mrs. Stumplemeyer called her scouts over to prepare for the event, and the girls from Troop 7 left, looking over their shoulders at Becca and snickering.

"Don't let them bother you," Jonnie said, squeezing Becca's

shoulder. "They're just trying to psych us out so they have a better chance of winning."

Jonnie was right. Becca smiled at her confidently. She wanted Troop 13 to win the Jamboree now more than ever.

Soon Troop 13 was called to the cave entrance.

"All right, girls," said Mrs. Stumplemeyer. "Good luck. And remember, if you get scared or have any problems, blow your whistle and the closest ranger will find you. There's no shame in giving up if you can't do it."

Becca caught Susan glaring at Mrs. Stumplemeyer. Susan leaned in to give the girls a pep talk.

"Scouts, you're going to do just fine in there," Susan said softly. "Stay calm, and remember you've got plenty of scouting skills. Just think through the questions carefully before you answer them. They may be kind of tricky."

All eight girls from Troop 13 lined up. Mrs. Stumplemeyer stared at her stopwatch for several seconds, then blew another ear-piercing whistle.

Troop 13 was off.

Sierra led them to an opening the size of an extra-large pizza. She squeezed through, followed by CJ, then Becca and Jonnie. The last four girls brought up the rear.

Becca inhaled the dank air and shined her headlight around the tiny cave. Crystals glinted just a foot overhead, and leaflike rock formations decorated the floor and walls. The place smelled musty and damp, like her basement. It gave her the creeps.

"Okay, guys, listen." CJ shined her headlight on the map. "Here's the first question: 'Why does Buddha contemplate his navel?'" CJ looked quizzically at Becca. "What the heck is that supposed to mean?"

Becca shook her head. "You should know this one, CJ."

"Why? 'Cause I'm Vietnamese?" she snapped. "Just because I'm Asian doesn't mean I know everything about Asian culture!"

CJ's angry tone startled the troop. Becca was speechless.

"I think we're missing the point," said Sierra quickly. "Let's focus on what 'contemplate his navel' means."

"It means 'study your bellybutton,'" Jonnie replied. Everyone giggled and the tense mood seemed to lift.

"But what's that supposed to mean?" Courtney asked.

"It means if you focus on something, it's supposed to make you think better."

Jonnie received more puzzled looks.

"Well, let's keep going," Sierra said. "Something ahead will give us the answer." She led the scouts to another opening the size of a trash can lid.

Becca pulled CJ aside. "Listen, CJ, I'm sorry for what I said. I didn't mean—"

"It's all right," CJ cut in. "I guess I'm more nervous about this event than I expected. Let's just forget about it and move on, okay?"

Becca gave her a quick hug. "Okay."

The next cave was the size of a basketball court. More crystals hung from the ceiling and jutted from the ground. One wall looked like a frozen waterfall with white, foamy waves at the bottom. Giant blue and green mushrooms the size of small stools surrounded a little pond that glistened in the light from the girls' helmets.

"Look at the mushrooms!" CJ exclaimed, her mouth open in awe. "I wonder if they're poisonous."

Sierra laughed. "They aren't mushrooms. They're crystals, formed over thousands of years. Remember, we're not supposed to touch anything. So don't try biting off a piece."

"This cave could be a palace," thought Becca, "fit for a king—or better yet—a queen."

"There he is!" Sierra pointed to one side of the cave.

"There who is?" Becca saw only a large round stone.

"Buddha!"

Becca stared at the gigantic form. It did look just like the statue of Buddha she'd seen in her social studies book. A small head topped a large smooth belly that had giant hands and arms resting on it.

"So what's he supposed to be contemplating?" Jonnie asked. "He looks like he's just rubbing his belly."

"Maybe he's hungry," Jennifer offered.

"Or full," Melissa added.

CJ moved closer to get a better look. A shiny doughnut-shaped crystal rested around one the Buddha's fingers. She reached forward, but Sierra grabbed her wrist. "Don't touch it, CJ! You know the rules."

"I know, I know. Don't touch the geological formations." But something was funny about that crystal. Carefully she picked it up.

"CJ! What are you doing?" Sierra demanded.

"It's not a crystal."

"What do you mean?"

CJ held it up for all to see. "It's cloth. In fact...it's a scrunchy!"

"What? Why was it on Buddha?" Jonnie asked.

"I don't know. Is it part of our clue?" CJ read the question again.

Suddenly Becca gasped. "Tiffany!"

"Tiffany?" Melissa and Kelly said in unison.

"I recognize that material. It's the scrunchy Tiffany was wearing this morning."

"But why was it on Buddha?" Jonnie asked.

"So we'd miss the real clue and get the answer wrong," CJ reasoned. She stepped closer to the Buddha and contemplated it. "I've got it! The scrunchy was covering up this hand, right? See what's sticking out underneath?"

The others looked puzzled.

Becca shrugged. "It's just a small crystal."

"And what does it look like when it's sticking out of his thumb?"

No one said anything.

"A splinter!" CJ exclaimed.

"CJ's right." said Becca. "Buddha isn't contemplating his navel after all. He has a splinter. A stalactite splinter."

"Stalagmite," Sierra corrected. "Stalactites hang down. Stalagmites go up."

"Stalagmite then. Anyway, Tiffany must have tried to hide it so we'd get the wrong answer."

"Come on, scouts," Sierra said. "No telling what's up ahead with Tiffany in front of us. Follow me; we're heading for the

Dragon's Lair." The girls followed Sierra through the next opening.

Becca brought up the rear. Dragon's Lair. She didn't like the sound of that.

Suddenly she stopped and listened for a second. She'd distinctly heard something.

A moan.

Chapter 5

"What was that?" Becca whispered to CJ.

"What was what?" CJ answered.

"That...moaning sound."

"I didn't hear anything."

"You didn't?" Becca turned around to check the cave but saw nothing in the light from her headlight. She wondered how close the park rangers were. "It sounded like somebody was sick or something. Kind of like crying but not exactly."

"Moaning, right," CJ confirmed.

"You sure you didn't hear it?" asked Becca.

CJ shook her head. "Maybe what you heard was Tiffany, just before she fell into a bottomless pit."

Becca rolled her eyes.

"We can dream, can't we?" CJ turned back to follow the troop. Becca hesitated for another second, then shivered and moved on.

With Sierra leading the way, the scouts easily found their way through the rest of the caves listed on the map: the Dragon's Breath, the Spikes and Spires, the Flames of Fire, and the Diamond Dome. And with CJ's expertise, they solved the puzzles quickly. As Troop 13 stepped into the sunshine, Becca was certain they'd won the event in record time.

Unfortunately, the troop leaders wouldn't announce which troop won until the award ceremony that evening. Becca hated the suspense, but she'd just have to wait.

When the tired, muddy scouts from Troop 13 trudged into camp, Becca noticed most of the other troops had already finished their snacks and were preparing for the last event, the nonviolent animal trap.

"We won't lose again because of me," Becca promised herself, munching her trail mix. She was ready this time, thanks to the information she'd found on the Internet.

After straightening up their campsites and changing into clean T-shirts and shorts, the scouts hiked to a clearing near the caves.

"Giiirrlllls!" Mrs. Stumplemeyer screeched, even though everyone was already there. She blew her whistle to make sure all eyes were on her. Becca sighed.

"As you know, this is our final event of the Jamboree. Like last year, you're to create a trap that will catch an animal without harming it. The troop that first catches an animal wins the event. Last year Troop 7 won, after Troop 13 was disqualified for...well, never mind."

The scouts giggled at the reference to Mrs. Stumplemeyer's fall from grace and into Troop 13's trap. Becca blushed furiously remembering the incident. When she'd called Mrs. Stumplemeyer over to check the trap, she should have warned the troop leader to step around the branches covering the pit. But Becca had been so wrapped up in making sure the pit wouldn't harm an animal that the trap ended up harming Mrs. Stumplemeyer—or at least her pride.

During the time Troop 13 had to waste helping the bulky woman out of the hole and resetting the trap, Troop 7 had managed to catch a rabbit. Although CJ had tried to argue that Mrs. Stumplemeyer was technically an animal, the troop leaders had disagreed and declared Troop 7 the winner.

This year, though, their trap wouldn't be a pit. Becca didn't want to take any chances. She'd feel awful if they lost again, but she knew she'd feel even worse if her trap harmed an animal—even if it was Mrs. Stumplemeyer.

"You have two hours to build your trap," Mrs. Stumplemeyer continued. "When you hear the whistle, you're to hide in the bushes and wait for an animal to find the bait and get caught. The first troop to trap an animal blows a whistle. The troop leaders will come see what you've caught."

"If you've caught an acceptable animal," she looked pointedly at Becca, "the other troops will be alerted, and then we'll announce the winner. During the ceremony tonight, we'll award the gold medal to the troop that's won the most events."

Tiffany sauntered over to Becca and her friends, her ponytail swinging with each step. "Who are you going to trap this year, dorks? A ranger? The boogieman? Or maybe yourselves!"

Tiffany's troopmates laughed while the girls from Troop 13 glared.

"You've heard the news, haven't you?" Tiffany asked.

Becca shrugged. "What, that you're going to lose this year?"

"Not even! We've got a great trap planned. My father knows someone who leads real safaris, and he gave us a blueprint for this awesome trap."

"Yeah, right. Well, we aren't in the jungle, so I hope you weren't counting on catching a lion or something."

"As a matter of fact," Tiffany said, smiling phonily, "I am."

"Am what?" CJ asked.

"Counting on catching a lion. Haven't you heard the rumors?"

"We don't listen to rumors," Sierra answered coolly.

"Well, you might want to hear this one. I heard a couple of the rangers talking, and one of them said he thought he saw a mountain lion last night."

"Yeah, sure," said Sierra. CJ and Jonnie shook their heads in disgust, blowing her off. But Becca said nothing. Mountain lion? She felt tiny beads of sweat break out on her forehead.

"If there were a mountain lion, we'd all be on buses heading home," CJ said. The girls from Troop 13 agreed. Becca forced a nod.

"Well, I'm just warning you. It hasn't been confirmed, but I'm not going to take any chances with my trap," Tiffany said. "And besides, if there is a mountain lion, we plan on catching it. Then we'll be heroes." The girls from Troop 7 nodded smugly.

Before the four friends could respond, Mrs. Stumplemeyer blew her whistle. The scouts hustled to their assigned areas to begin constructing their traps.

"What have you got for us this year, Bec?" Sierra asked.

Becca sat on a log and studied her printout of the plans. "Every year we all dig the same old leaf-covered pits. This year we're going to build a trap completely different from everyone else's."

"How?"

"Instead of going down, the animal will go up," Becca said mysteriously.

"How is it going to do that?" Jonnie asked.

"See those four trees over there?" The girls glanced at the trees that marked off a ten-foot-square patch of ground. "We're going to throw ropes over the branches. Jonnie, are you up for some more climbing?"

Jonnie nodded.

Becca continued, "We'll dig a small, shallow pit in the middle, then spread a net over it."

"I get it!" CJ said. "The animal will step into the hole and trigger the trap. It'll be caught in the net and swing from the trees. But wait...how are you going to get the ropes to pull up the net?"

"See those four rocks about the size of watermelons? We'll tie rope around each one and prop the rocks in the trees. When the animal steps onto the net, the net will be dragged down by its weight, which will pull on the ropes and cause the rocks to fall."

"And that will make the net trap the animal in a hammock!" Sierra said. "Cool!"

The scouts buzzed with excitement as they got to work. While Becca, Jonnie, and Courtney dug the pit, CJ, Sierra, and Melissa hauled over the four rocks. Jennifer and Kelly gathered the ropes and net from the troop leaders. Within an hour, the trap was ready to be set.

"Jonnie, tie this rope around your ankle," Becca directed. "Then climb about ten feet and throw the rope over a branch that's a little higher. When the rope falls to us, we'll tie it around the rock and hoist it to you. Then you balance the rock between the trunk and the branch you're sitting on. Okay?"

Jonnie scurried up the tree. When she got hold of the rock, she carefully shifted around so she could prop it against the trunk.

CJ watched Jonnie balance the rock so it'd fall if the rope jerked. "Does it matter which way it falls?" she asked.

"No," Becca answered. "All the rocks will fall straight down about halfway to the ground, and that's what will make the net scoop up the animal."

In forty-five minutes, all four rocks were set in the trees, the net was tied to the free ends of rope and laid over the shallow hole, and leaves were scattered over the net to hide it. After setting out the bait, the eight scouts from Troop 13 were ready for business.

Becca glanced around to see what traps their competitors had rigged. Amber's troop, Troop 10, had constructed the usual pit trap, as had several other troops. Troop 7 had hung blankets around their trap. Becca was curious what they'd come up with, but she felt certain her troop's trap was going to be the best. Of course, that's what she'd thought last year.

A few minutes later Mrs. Stumplemeyer came into view and blew her whistle to start the final event.

"All right, scouts! It's time to hide and wait for your traps to be triggered. I'll come around and check each one to make sure it won't harm animals. We wouldn't want anything—or anyone—to get hurt." Mrs. Stumplemeyer glared at Becca again.

After Mrs. Stumplemeyer approved all the other traps (even Troop 13's), she arrived at the last one. The girls from Troop 7 dramatically pulled off the blankets and stood back to let their troop leader admire their work.

"What do we have here, Tiffany?" Mrs. Stumplemeyer said grandly, as if she didn't already know. She was, after all, their troop leader.

"Well, Mrs. Stumplemeyer, we've made a professional lion trap just like safari guides use. We made a cage out of branches and twine, and when the animal goes into it to eat the bait, one of us waiting up in the tree releases this rope. That lets the door to the cage close and the animal is trapped!" Tiffany beamed.

"Very clever, scouts," gushed Mrs. Stumplemeyer.

Becca had to agree the trap *was* pretty cool, but she still thought hers was better.

"It's time to take your places, scouts," Mrs. Stumplemeyer announced. "This takes patience, so I hope you came prepared to wait."

The girls hid close enough to see their traps but far away enough so the animals couldn't sense them. Each scout brought something quiet to do during the wait. Sierra helped CJ practice sign language. Jonnie read a book about climbing Mount Everest. Courtney, Kelly, Jennifer, and Melissa read mysteries or played cat's cradle. Everyone seemed relaxed.

Everyone except Becca. Her eyes scanned the bushes, watchful of any movement in them. She turned to Jonnie and whispered, "Do you think it's true?"

"What?" Jonnie whispered back.

"The rumor about the mountain lion. Do you think there really is one around here?"

Jonnie shrugged. "I doubt it. The rangers would have sent us home. Or at least would have told us so we'd be careful. I'm sure Tiffany made it up. You know she's trying to psych us out."

Becca nodded. "Still, what if it is true?" she persisted, but Jonnie had already gone back to her book.

Becca plucked a strand of grass and stuck an end in her mouth. It dangled from her lips as she watched the trap intently, glancing at the surrounding area every few minutes. The rangers *had* said there were all kinds of animals in the area…and lots of them. She visualized the mountain lion approaching their trap, then getting caught. Tiffany was right. They'd be heroes if they actually caught a mountain lion!

Suddenly she heard a noise behind her, and she whipped her head toward the sound. And then she saw it swishing behind the dense manzanita bushes. A tuft of fur on top of a long, light golden brown tail. It looked just like a mountain lion's tail.

Before Becca could say anything, she heard a whooshing noise.

"Whoa!" CJ yelled.

Becca jumped up, half-expecting to find a mountain lion about to eat CJ. But CJ was running toward the trap. The rest of the girls quickly followed.

Becca peeked back at the bushes. The tail was gone. Had she imagined it?

Spooked, Becca rushed to join her troopmates. She glanced back several times, just to make sure nothing was hot on her heels.

Chapter 6

"Look!" Sierra squealed. "We caught something! We caught something!" She jumped up and down and hugged Jonnie. Both giggled as they strained to see what was trapped.

Susan came running over. "What is it?" she asked, peering at the net swinging about six feet from the ground.

"I think it's a fox," said Courtney.

"A raccoon," said Jennifer.

"A beaver," offered Kelly.

The girls surrounded the net, waiting for the other leaders to verify their capture—and declare them the winners of the event.

"We won! We won!" Sierra repeated, hugging CJ, then Becca, then the rest of the troop.

Girls from the other troops began arriving to see the captured critter wiggling inside the leaf-lined net.

Mrs. Stumplemeyer finally arrived, breathing hard from the trek from her troop's hiding place. She tried to blow her whistle, but only air and spit came out. Once she caught her breath, she began giving orders.

"All right scouts, settle down. Settle!" The girls quieted, eager for the unveiling. "Ranger Bruce will be here in a minute. He'll free the animal, and we'll see what you girls have caught."

Ranger Bruce arrived with Ranger Christine. He carried a

cage while she held a canvas bag large enough to contain a small animal.

"Scouts, I want you to move back, way back," Ranger Bruce said. "Animals in the wild aren't like your pets. Some could have rabies or other diseases. When I lower the trap, I want to contain the animal and place it in a cage. We'll set it free far from the camp."

The girls reluctantly backed away as the rangers slowly lowered the net. When it landed on the ground, it fell open and revealed the small, frightened animal.

Everyone froze.

The animal lifted its tail.

The smell hit the crowd's nostrils before they even had time to think.

"Eeeeeuuuwwwww!"

"Run for your life!"

"SKUNK!!!"

The scouts cleared out in a matter of seconds, leaving the rangers holding their equipment. Screams carried into the distance, as mass hysteria gripped the crowd. Even Mrs. Stumplemeyer tried to flee the noxious odor.

Unfortunately, she tripped on a tree root after taking five steps.

The skunk caught up with her before she could even lift her head. It lifted its tail, aimed, and fired.

Over dinner of beef stew in sourdough bread, hot apple cider, and more s'mores, the scouts from Troop 13 talked about the events, how well they did, and what they'd do differently next year.

But most of all, they giggled about what happened to Mrs. Stumplemeyer. Luckily for her, the rangers kept all kinds of remedies on hand: snakebite kits, poison oak soap, and skunk deodorizers. Yet after all those tomato juice baths and showers with lye soap, Mrs. Stumplemeyer still smelled of skunk.

"You can't even smell the pine trees anymore around her," Becca joked.

When dinner was over, the troop leaders gathered everyone around the campfire for the award ceremony.

"Scouts," Susan began. She had replaced Mrs. Stumplemeyer, who was resting in her tent, as emcee. The troops quieted down.

"Before I announce the winners of this year's Jamboree, here's a recap of the event winners: Rappelling event: Troop 7."

The scouts from Troop 7 high-fived one another.

"Nonviolent animal trapping event: Troop 13."

Becca's troopmates grinned at her.

"And finally, the winners of the combined spelunking/problem solving event, who made their way through the caves and correctly answered all of the questions in fifty-three minutes and six seconds..."

CJ, Sierra, Jonnie, and Becca grasped one another's hands.

"Troop 13!"

The four friends squealed, then joined their troopmates in a group hug. They'd won!

Susan continued, "I am proud to present this year's gold medal to the members of Troop 13, for their creative use of scouting skills, their individual talents, and especially for their overall teamwork. Congratulations!"

The girls from Troop 13 walked to the front of the crowd. They tried to look serious but were unable to suppress their smiles. Each proudly shook Susan's hand and beamed as a gold medal was placed around her neck. Applause thundered from the other troops, who hugged and high-fived the winning scouts.

Except for Troop 7, Becca noticed. Those girls had disappeared.

"I have another surprise, scouts," announced Susan when the congratulations died down. "Instead of the usual campfire songs and ghost stories tonight, we're going into town to visit a gold-mining museum. I thought you all might want to learn how to pan for gold so you could try your luck tomorrow during your free day."

Another cheer went up. The girls scrambled to their tents to prepare for the trip to town. While Sierra, CJ, and Jonnie changed into jeans, Becca headed for her laptop.

"What are you doing, Becca?" asked CJ. "You're coming with us, aren't you?"

Becca nodded absently. "Yeah, I just want to check something..." She focused on the screen.

"What are you looking for?" Sierra leaned over Becca's shoulder. "More stuff about that lost gold?"

Becca shrugged. "Maybe."

In a few minutes, Susan called, "Time to go. Everyone ready?"

Jonnie, CJ, and Sierra scampered out of the tent. Becca shut down the laptop. "Shoot," she whispered.

"Find anything more about the gold?" Jonnie asked when Becca joined them.

She shook her head. "Not enough time. I'll try again tonight."

"Let's go!" Susan said. As the girls followed Susan in pairs, they sang a song appropriate for the gold country:

Make new friends,
But keep the old.
One is silver,
And the other's gold!

Naturally CJ sang her own version, which quickly caught on:

Meet new boys,
But keep the rest.
New one's cuter,
But the old one's best!

In twenty minutes they arrived at the Nugget Museum in Flat Skunk, right in the heart of the gold country.

"Scouts," Susan said at the bottom of the museum steps. "You'll be interested to know that this tiny town was once a popular center for prospectors. More than thirty tons of gold were mined from nearby caves, including the Haunted Caves. If you look around, you might see some of the descendants of the original miners."

"It looks like a ghost town," Sierra whispered as she surveyed the dilapidated buildings, wooden plank sidewalks, and boarded windows. Besides the Nugget Museum, the only other businesses seemed to be a video store/bait shop and a half-dozen antique stores.

"Not much here now, that's for sure," said Becca. They climbed the rickety steps to the museum's front porch.

"It's creeping me out," added Jonnie, bouncing on a squeaky step.

Just as they reached the porch, the door flew open with a loud screech.

The scouts jumped. Several screamed. Becca's heart pounded in her chest.

Staring down at them from the doorway was a giant scarecrow. It had a crusty, old face made of worn and wrinkled leather, olive-black eyes, and a hideous toothless grin. Its sparse gray hair stuck up like porcupine quills. Its bony arms and legs were dressed mostly in rags, and its shoes were caked with mud.

For a moment, Becca thought it was the best scarecrow she'd ever seen. But then it opened its mouth.

Chapter 7

"Welcome!" said the scarecrow.

The scouts gasped.

Just then, an old man appeared at the door. Grinning toothily, he tapped the scarecrow on the shoulder and handed it a glass of water. The scarecrow reached into the glass, pulled out something floating inside, and slipped it into its mouth.

It smiled again, this time with a full set of teeth.

"Scared ya, didn't he?" the man said, patting the scarecrow on the back. "Heh heh. Sluice gets 'em every time. Well, come on in. I'm Winky Pike, museum curator. An' I got lots more to show ya."

He opened the door wide and stood back. The girls hesitated a moment, then cautiously entered the Nugget Museum. Becca wondered if the two men were descendants of miners. They were so old and weathered, they looked as if they could have been original forty-niners.

At the hands-on exhibit, another old prospector named Panner, who was huge and had an enormous head, helped the scouts practice panning for gold. After swirling and pouring water through a homemade sluice that looked like a slanted water trough, each scout got to keep enough gold flakes to cover her pinkie fingernail.

While the girls panned or read through the pamphlets on Black Bart and the World's Biggest Nugget, Winky told stories about his days as a prospector.

"Me and Sluice and Panner over there all come from Kentucky to strike it rich. That was durin' the Rush of '39. Been here ever since," said Winky. Sluice clicked his false teeth, which he'd kept in during the tour, to Becca's relief.

"There was another gold rush in 1939?" Courtney asked.

"Heck, yeah. There've been a bunch of 'em. Every decade or so, someone strikes a new vein."

"Did you find gold?" CJ examined the tiny gold flakes on her finger as if they were magic beans.

"Nope," Winky said, shaking his head glumly. He glanced over at Sluice and Panner. "We was just a bunch of dime store miners, like most everyone else, hopin' to strike it rich. Never happened."

"Is there any gold left?" Jonnie asked.

"Oh, there's plenty still. It's just too hard to get to, buried deep in the caves or sunk low in the creek beds. We make our gold off the tourists now, leadin' panning expeditions and such."

Becca spoke up for the first time. "Have you ever heard of Black Bart's lost gold?"

The three men looked at one another then grinned. Winky shook his head. "That old tale. It'll never die. One of them rural legends, you might say. The gold probably don't exist—at least no one's ever found it so far. Me and Sluice and Panner went lookin' for it some years back out at the Haunted Caves, we but never found nothin'. Except this here watch!"

He held up his wrist and showed off a sports watch that told time in three time zones, had an alarm, and glowed in the dark.

"I guess one of the tourists dropped it. Too bad; it's a nice watch."

Becca nodded, then added, "I found this poem on the Internet about Black Bart's gold. Have you read it?"

Winky nodded. "We don't have no computer, but I probably seen it somewhere. Got a whole collection of his poems right here." Winky reached behind him and grabbed a handful of small booklets. He sifted through a Bret Harte collection of short stories, Mark Twain's "The Celebrated Jumping Frog of Calaveras County," and a history of Joaquin Murietta. At last he found the poems by Black Bart. He handed the booklet to Becca.

"Wish I'd studied poetry," Winky said. "Maybe I could figure out what he was tryin' to say in all them poems. Maybe there's some kind of clue to his hidden treasure, like the story goes. But I never got nothin' from any of 'em, except confused. Keep that if you want. Maybe you can explain it to me one day."

"Thanks," Becca said, flipping through the pages. She checked the table of contents. "That's odd. The poem from the Internet isn't listed."

"He wrote a bunch of poems. Probably couldn't fit them all in one little booklet. Right, boys?" Winky glanced at his pals. Becca turned and caught them staring at her before they quickly looked away. "Creepy," she thought.

"Time to head back, scouts," Susan said. "The sun is nearly down, and it's going to be dark soon."

Becca suddenly thought of the mountain lion. She'd have to

look up mountain lions on the Internet and see what their habits were. Did they roam at night? Were they afraid of humans? Did they prefer blond girls to redheads and brunettes?

"Good luck in yer search for the gold, girls," Winky said, showing the scouts to the door. "Come by any time if you have questions. Sluice and Panner and me will be glad to answer 'em. An' if you decide to go lookin' for gold in them caves, we got some equipment you might want to borrow."

The girls followed Susan back up the path toward camp, singing songs and waving their flashlights. Darkness was almost upon them, but it looked as if they'd have a full moon tonight. The moonbeams would light up the camp like a stadium.

"Becca, you haven't said a word since we left the museum," said CJ, unzipping the tent door. "What have you been—"

"What's that?" Becca interrupted, pointing to the top of the tent.

CJ squinted. "Looks like a piece of cloth." She took a step into the tent and froze. Inhaling quickly she whispered, "Oh my gosh!"

The other girls peered cautiously inside. Becca half-expected to see a mountain lion—or worse, the skunk—but knew CJ wouldn't still be standing there if that were the case. She silently surveyed the tent with her flashlight. "Oh my gosh!" she echoed CJ, stunned.

Someone had tied all their clothes together and strung them from the ceiling. The inside looked like a circus tent with colorful cloth ropes hung all around. Even their sleeping bags had been tied into giant knots.

CJ yanked down one of the knotted ropes. "My favorite sweatshirt!" She pulled at the knots, but they didn't loosen easily.

When she finally got them undone, she held it up. "I mean this *was* my favorite sweatshirt." It now looked like a wadded-up rag that had been batted around by a mountain lion.

"Tiffany!" Becca deduced, gritting her teeth.

For the next forty-five minutes, the girls said nothing as they untied their clothes. After slipping into their pajamas and packing the rest of the clothes in their backpacks, the girls sank into their sleeping bags, exhausted.

Except for Becca. She was going through her clothes a second time.

"What's the matter, Becca? Is something missing?" Jonnie propped herself up on her elbows.

Becca glanced around the tent and put her hands on her hips. "Yeah, my under—oh no!"

Becca bolted from the tent, scanned the area, then looked up at trees. There were her underpants, waving in the cool night breeze for all to see at the crack of dawn. How did they get up there? And how was she supposed to get them down?

Jonnie, CJ, and Sierra clambered out of the tent.

"What is it?" Sierra asked.

Becca pointed.

"Oh no!" CJ said. "Not your—"

"Underpants!" Jonnie finished the sentence.

The four girls looked at each other then back at the clothing decorating the branches.

"Tiffany," they said in unison.

Chapter 8

"Well, I'm not going to bed until I get my underpants down!" said Becca.

CJ, Jonnie, and Sierra stared at her in shock. Then all four burst out laughing.

"That's not what I meant!" she explained as the laughter died down. "I meant I have to get them down from the trees, you dorks! Everyone will see them in the morning!"

Becca bowed her head. Her three friends realized then she was really upset and rallied around her.

"Don't worry, Bec," said CJ. "We'll get them down. All for one, and one for all, remember?"

"That's the Three Musketeers, CJ, not the scouts." Becca wiped her eyes.

"Well, we're the Four...Scout-a-teers!"

The three gave CJ an impatient look.

"That's not even a word!" said Sierra.

"Okay, how about the Fearsome Four?"

Three shaking heads.

"Fantastic Four?" CJ tried again.

Rolled eyes this time.

"Fine. Forget about it," she scowled.

"That's it!" shouted Jonnie. "We'll be the Forget-about-It Four!"

The girls hooked pinkies to lock in their new name. Then they set about retrieving Becca's underpants.

"Jonnie and I will climb those trees and try to unhook the underpants caught on the branches," Sierra said. She pointed to a couple of tall pines. "You guys throw some pine cones at the ones farther up those trees. Maybe if you hit them they'll fall down."

"Keep an eye out for Susan. She thinks we're getting ready for bed," warned Jonnie.

As Jonnie and Sierra climbed the trees, CJ and Becca began throwing pine cones.

"Hey, watch it, CJ!" Jonnie called down. "You almost knocked *me* out of the tree with that last one!"

After several more attempts, Becca and CJ managed to hit the branches that had the underpants. Becca watched with a mixture of joy and horror as her most embarrassing clothing fluttered down like giant silky butterflies.

"What are you girls doing up?"

Becca whirled around to face Susan. "Great lookout I make," she thought. Susan stood with her hands on her hips, trying to look stern but not quite hiding her smile.

"Uh, nothing, Susan! Just...getting my clothes," Becca stammered. She tried hard not to look at Jonnie and Sierra in the trees. "Right, CJ?" She didn't trust CJ to keep quiet and shot her a warning look.

CJ looked away from the trees just before Susan caught her eye.

"Why did you throw my clothes out of the tent, you dork?" Becca asked CJ, forcing a laugh. It sounded so fake.

CJ managed a smile and shrugged, catching Becca's meaning.

"Yeah, we were just goofing around. Sorry, Susan," she said.

"Well, go to bed. You're going to be too tired to enjoy your free time tomorrow if you don't get some sleep. Besides..." Susan stepped over toward the girls' tent and started to peek inside. In a flash, Becca blocked the entrance.

"Shhh!" Becca said. "Jonnie and Sierra are asleep. We were trying not to wake them. That's why we were outside."

Susan stood up. "Well, you girls should be asleep, too. Now get in there. I'll see you in the morning."

Becca and CJ nodded. They held the tent door open as if about to enter, while Susan headed back to her tent.

Something fell softly on Becca's head.

"Girls?" Susan called from the darkness.

Becca snatched the object off her head and held it behind her back, ready to face Susan if she reappeared.

"Y...yes?" Becca answered.

"Don't forget to brush your teeth."

Becca clutched the underpants tightly behind her back.

"We already did," she called back.

Becca and CJ listened until the crunching of dried pine needles faded. They waited a full minute more before whispering to their tree-perched friends.

"Who? Who?" CJ called softly.

"What are you doing?" Becca whispered to CJ.

"I'm telling them the coast is clear," CJ whispered back, "in owl language."

Becca shook her head. "Why are you using owl language?"

"'Cause it's too dark to use sign language."

There was no point in arguing with CJ. She used her own logic. Maybe that's what made her such an expert puzzle-solver.

In a matter of minutes, Jonnie and Sierra were on the ground, bringing a shower of pine needles with them.

"That was a close one!" Jonnie whispered, wiping her palms on her pants.

"Yeah, and dropping my underpants on my head didn't help! You almost got us caught!" Becca hissed.

"Where did Susan come from anyway?" Sierra said softly. "I thought we were being quiet."

"Well, let's not take any more chances," Becca said. "Everyone in the tent, before she starts sleepwalking or something."

The scouts followed Becca inside and snuggled into their cool beds. Jonnie and Sierra were out like lights the moment their heads hit their pillows. CJ worked on a crossword puzzle for a few minutes before clicking off her flashlight.

Only Becca stayed awake for another half-hour, unable to relax. Her mind drifted back to the Nugget Museum and the words of Winky Pike. She sat up, dug through her backpack, and pulled out the booklet of poems the old prospector had given her. By the glow of her flashlight, she read the entire booklet.

And she still couldn't get to sleep. If reading a bunch of mediocre poems couldn't put her to sleep, what would?

Becca sat up again and reached for her laptop. She waited for the Internet connection then headed for the web site on Black Bart that she had bookmarked. There she reread the legend of the "Gentleman Robber," who was so polite, he apologized to the victims after robbing them. And he never shot anyone.

"That was very polite," Becca thought sarcastically. "It sure would be rude to shoot someone."

Becca clicked onto to the Camp Miwok web site and studied the layout of the Haunted Caves. As she mentally traveled through the caves, she tried to imagine where Black Bart might have hidden his fortune. Maybe in one of the caves or tunnels she crawled through this afternoon? She pictured them as she read the names: Devil's Dungeon, Flames of Fire, Toadstool Tunnel...

Becca remembered Toadstool Tunnel, where the geological formations looked like giant mushrooms. But her troop hadn't gone into Devil's Dungeon. Becca wondered what it looked like. Probably had a couple of devil's horns sticking above the entrance, with some stalagmites that looked like flames or something inside. And what about Flames of Fire? They hadn't gone in there either.

Becca suddenly thought something sounded familiar. Devil's Dungeon and Flames of Fire. Those were phrases Black Bart used in one of his poems. But not in a poem found in the booklet Winky had given her—in the one she'd found on the Internet.

Becca backtracked until she reached the Black Bart web site. She scrolled down through the story and pictures until she reached the poem. She read it to herself again, slowly this time:

Beware you eager miners,
Looking for the gold,
All you'll find are moaners,
Chilled from crystal cold.
Keep on cascade climbing,
Bet on flames of fire,

Ask for devil's dungeons,
risk the spikes and spire.
Toadstool tunnels dead end,
Coral cove is bare;
All the cavern's empty,
Venture if you dare.
End up here—but where?

What an odd poem. It was as if Black Bart wanted the reader to think there was treasure in the Haunted Caves. But what did the clues mean? The names in the poem matched the cave names, but they weren't listed in any particular order. And they didn't seem to lead anywhere specific.

"'End up here,'" Becca repeated. But where?

After reading the poem a third time, Becca was sure it was a code to the hidden loot. But she couldn't figure out how to crack it. She'd have to show it to CJ first thing in the morning. Maybe the puzzle expert could make something out of it.

Becca shut down her laptop and snuggled into her sleeping bag. It took her a while to fall asleep, and when she did, she dreamed of dragons and devils and dungeons and fire.

She woke up in a sweat, just as she was about to find Black Bart's gold.

Chapter 9

The next morning Becca was back at her laptop before any of the other girls had stirred. But the clicking of the keys and Becca's muttering eventually woke CJ.

"Beccaaaa. What are you doing?" CJ groaned from inside her sleeping bag.

"CJ! Come here!" Becca tried to whisper, but she was too excited to keep quiet. She watched Jonnie and Sierra roll in their sleeping bags. CJ peeked out from hers.

"What? More underpants in the trees? If they're not mine, I'm going back to sleep."

"No, you're not. I have something to show you, and I need your help. It's a...puzzle. And I can't figure it out."

CJ's eyes opened wide. Becca knew all it would take was the challenge of a cryptic puzzle to wake up her friend. CJ wiggled out of her sleeping bag, crawled over to Becca, and peered at the laptop screen.

"I hate poetry," she groaned.

Becca shook her head. "This isn't a poem. Well, it is, but I think it's really some kind of coded message. It might have something to do with where Black Bart's treasure is hidden. Read it."

CJ read the poem aloud. By now, Sierra was sitting up in her sleeping bag, and Jonnie was awake but not up.

"Yeah, it's a poem, all right," CJ confirmed when she finished. "There, I solved the mystery."

"No, CJ, it's not just a poem. Look at this map." Becca pulled out a brochure map of the Haunted Caves. "Devil's Dungeon, Coral Cove, Cascade Climb, Spikes and Spires. They're all names of the caves."

"So?" said CJ. "You didn't need me to tell you that."

Sierra reached over and took the map from Becca. "Let me see." She loved maps and had a Mapping Your Way badge. She always followed the route on a map every time the troop went on a field trip.

"Read it again, CJ," Becca insisted. "I think there's something in this poem that connects it to the map. Black Bart is trying to tell us where the gold is. I'm sure of it."

When CJ finished, Jonnie said, "There *is* something odd about that poem. It's off a line."

Becca counted the lines in the poem and nodded. "You're right. It has an extra line, doesn't it? That's weird." Thirteen lines. Interesting. Just like Troop 13.

"Read those names again," Sierra said, still studying the map. CJ did.

"Hmmm," Sierra said distractedly.

"What?" asked Becca.

Sierra shrugged. "Nothing. It's just odd that the poem mentions every cave listed on the map except Black Bart Cave and Black Bat Cave."

Jonnie sat up on one elbow. "Maybe they weren't discovered until recently—after Black Bart wrote that poem and after he hid his gold. If there is any gold. Besides, Black Bat Cave looks like it was just discovered. It's not even open to the public."

The four girls sat quietly for a few minutes, each lost in her own thoughts.

Becca finally spoke. "I say we bring the map and the poem and try to make some sense of it while we're in the caves."

"Great idea," said Jonnie. "We've got all day to explore them on our own. Maybe once we get there, we'll find something that will help us figure out the secret."

"If there is a secret," CJ reminded them. "We still don't know if there is any gold."

Becca nodded. "True, but it'll still be fun to search for it. Right?" The girls agreed and quickly pulled on their jeans and T-shirts.

After a breakfast of one-eyed omelets, cheesy breadsticks, griddle bacon, and hot cocoa with miniature marshmallows and cinnamon candies, the scouts from Troop 13 cleaned up their campsite, grabbed their coveralls and helmets from their tents, and gathered with the rest of the troops at the camp entrance.

"Girls!" Susan waved her scouts over. "Girls, you know the rules. Stay in pairs, keep your flashlights and whistles handy, and don't enter any of the caves that are roped off. They could be dangerous, since they haven't been renovated by the park system yet. Don't touch or take anything in the caves. And be here for lunch at noon. All right?"

The scouts nodded and mumbled agreement. As they hiked to the Haunted Caves, they sang their favorite tune:

The worms crawl in,
The worms crawl out,
The worms crawl over
your face and snout.
Your eyes bulge out,
Your teeth turn green,
Your pus runs out
like a molten stream...

Susan glanced back once, but her exasperated look just made the girls laugh and sing louder. It wasn't long before Becca heard Susan join in.

Troop 13 arrived at the caves' entrance and found Mrs. Stumplemeyer sitting nearby in a folding chair, reading a mystery novel. The scouts from Troop 7 had decided to spend their free day exploring the caves, too. "They're already inside," she said with a slight smirk.

"Shoot! They beat us!" CJ said as the girls crawled into their coveralls and adjusted their helmets.

"They're probably setting all kinds of booby traps," Jonnie said.

"Or they're hiding and planning to jump out and scare us," added Sierra.

Becca looked pointedly at them. "Or they're looking for Black Bart's gold."

"You think they know about it?" CJ asked.

"The legend is mentioned in the brochure," Becca said. "Everyone knows about the story. And Tiffany did refer to it."

"But they don't have the poem," said Jonnie.

Becca shrugged. "Yeah, well, we may have the poem, but we don't know what it means yet—"

Susan interrupted, "Courtney, Jennifer, Kelly, and Melissa, you're in one group. Becca, CJ, Jonnie, and Sierra, you're in another. Stay in your groups! See you at lunch time." She saluted them, and the scouts headed inside the dark, cold caves.

After an hour of exploring the winding tunnels and hidden rooms full of geological formations, tiny pools, crystalline figures, and glittering stones, the four girls rested on a large rock in Coral Co

and there's no sign of where Bla   gold," said Jonnie.

ap out of her fanny pack. "I'm still   at holds the key. Take another look

CJ read the poem aloud. Just as she finished, the girls heard an eerie sound.

"What was that?" CJ jumped up, dropping the poem and map to the ground.

The girls listened. Nothing.

"Our imagination," said Becca. "We probably heard—"

They heard something low-pitched, drawn out, and definitely creepy. A moan.

"There it is again!" CJ said. "I told you I heard something!"

Becca shushed her. They listened again.

"Ooooooooooooooooo," moaned the—what? Wind? Ghost?

Becca stood up. "I'll bet it's just Tiffany and her friends. They're trying to scare us out of here so they can have the place all to themselves." Becca cupped her mouth with her hands and yelled toward the cave entrance, "YOU'RE SO SCARY, TIFFANY!"

Her words echoed several more times.

"Yeah, you're right," said Sierra. "What a bunch of dorks they are."

CJ bent down to pick up the poem and map—and froze. "Oh my gosh! I've got it!" She pointed to the map lying on top of the poem. Only a few letters of the poem were uncovered.

"What is it?" Becca's eyes followed CJ's finger.

"The poem! See the letters that are showing?"

"Yeah, so?"

"I couldn't see it before when I was reading the poem normally like you're supposed to. But when all but the first letter of each line is covered, the words really jump out at you."

"What words?" asked Jonnie, straining to see what CJ saw.

"The coded message!"

Becca bent closer. "Oh my gosh!"

"What?" Jonnie cried.

"Read the first letter of each line," Becca said.

Jonnie sounded out the letters. "'B-L-A-C-K-B-A-R-T-C-A-V-E.' Black Bart Cave!" She snatched the map from the ground and opened it. "That's it! I see it! Black Bart's Cave!"

"Oh my gosh!" the girls screamed in unison. "That's got to be where the gold is hidden!"

In their excitement, the scouts never noticed the shadows lurking—and listening—just outside Coral Cove. That is, until they heard giggling and the trampling of feet.

Chapter 10

"They heard everything!" Becca said after giving up the chase to find the girls from Troop 7. A shiver ran up her spine.

"So?" said CJ. "They won't find anything. They don't have our brains."

"And all we have to do," added Jonnie, "is beat them to the cave. Let's go!"

The scouts followed the map to Black Bart Cave, taking the most direct route Sierra could find. But they weren't fast enough to beat Troop 7. Tiffany and her gang were waiting for them.

"What took you so long?" Tiffany relaxed on a large rock, trying to look as if she hadn't just raced to the cave.

"Yeah," mimicked Stephanie, a Tiffany clone. "We've been here for hours. Found the gold already, too." Tiffany held her hand out to show off the gold ring she'd gotten for her fourteenth birthday. Her friends burst into laughter.

"Yeah, right," said Becca, trying to hide her disappointment. Then she grinned. "We knew you'd fall for our little scheme."

Tiffany stiffened. "What scheme?"

Becca glanced at Sierra, Jonnie, and CJ. All three nodded, realizing what Becca was up to.

"We knew you were listening, so we made all that stuff up about Black Bart's gold," Jonnie said, getting into the game.

"And you walked right into our trap," added Sierra.

"What trap?" Gina looked around the cave.

"You'll see. While you all were spying on us and trying to find out about the gold, the rest of Troop 13 headed back to your camp."

"Why did they do that?" asked Tiffany.

The four girls from Troop 13 grinned. "Why do you think?" Becca asked innocently.

"Oh my gosh!" Tiffany jumped up, looking horrified. "They're doing something to our stuff! This was all a trick to distract us!"

Tiffany and her pals flew out of the cave like bats. In their hurry, they didn't hear the laughter echoing throughout the cave.

"Great, Becca! Now they're definitely out of our way." Jonnie patted her on the shoulder.

"At least for a while," said Becca. "But they'll be back when they realize we didn't do anything to their stuff. So we don't have much time. Let's start looking around and see if we can find anything that has to do with Black Bart's hidden treasure."

The girls scoured the cave, looking for signs of digging, maps on the walls, coded messages, or buried treasure. After thirty minutes, tired and discouraged, they gave up.

CJ studied the poem again, while Sierra scanned the map. Becca and Jonnie were lost in their thoughts. No one spoke for several minutes.

"Give me the poem, please, CJ," Becca said. "I want to read it one more time."

She took the paper from CJ and folded it to conceal all but the first letter of each line.

"There's something about this poem that isn't right. I'm not a poet, but we all know the basics of writing a poem from English class. And this one isn't...well...it isn't very good."

"So what?" said CJ. "He was a good robber. He didn't have to be a good poet."

"But his other poems aren't so bad," Becca said. "In this one, the meter is all off. And the line that starts with *r*. It's lowercase. All the rest are capitals. It's as if—"

CJ snatched the poem and finished Becca's thought. "That line doesn't belong."

"If we took it out, the poem would be even, with twelve lines. And all the lines would fit the pattern," Becca said, with renewed excitement.

CJ read the poem again. "And without it, it doesn't say 'BLACK BART CAVE' anymore." They looked at one another. "It says BLACK *BAT* CAVE."

Sierra held up the map again. "Black Bat Cave *is* on the map. But it's not open to the public yet." She stared at the three girls. "Do you think—"

Becca suddenly stood and put a finger to her lips. The girls listened hard for intruders. Jonnie tiptoed to the cave entrance, peeked out, and looked both ways. She shook her head. "No one there," she whispered.

"Come on!" Becca said. "Let's go find Black Bat Cave!"

After running into a couple of dead ends, Sierra finally led them to Black Bat Cave. Exhilarated, the girls ducked under an "Off Limits" sign and stepped into the cave—and were quickly disappointed.

"This place is teeny!" Jonnie stood on her tiptoes and touched the ceiling. "You can barely fit the four of us in here, especially with this boulder in the way."

"There aren't even any geological formations," Sierra complained. "It's just another cave with a big rock in it."

"And no gold," added CJ.

"Another wild goose chase," Jonnie sighed.

"There aren't even any bats!" CJ said.

Becca wasn't sorry about *that*. Even though Sierra said bats were gentle and important in nature, they totally creeped Becca out. She studied the small room, looking for any signs of hidden gold. Frowning, she pointed to the boulder. "Maybe there's something behind it."

"Well, let's just roll it over!" CJ teased. "Hope you've all been working out."

The four girls contemplated the boulder, which was the size of a big-screen TV. There was no way they'd be able to move it.

Sierra knelt and brushed her hand around the base of the rock.

"Turn your flashlights off," she said. "Since there's no electric lighting in this cave like there is in the others, it should be dark."

The girls switched off their flashlights, and the room went nearly pitch black.

"Okay, you can turn them back on now." Sierra stood up, looking disappointed.

"What were you looking for, Sierra?" Jonnie asked.

"Light. If this rock blocks an opening to another part of the cave, I thought there might be some light peeking through. But I didn't see any."

Jonnie squatted and ran her fingers as far around the base as she could. "Hmmm," she said. "Lift me up, will you, Sierra? I want to check around the top."

Sierra boosted her up, and Jonnie leaned and felt along the top edge.

"Yes!" she exclaimed, her body taut as she felt along the boulder.

"What is it?" CJ asked, trying to see on tiptoe.

"I feel cold air!" she said, excited.

"Duh, we know it's cold in here, Jonnie." CJ relaxed back on her heels and shook her head.

"No, this cold air is coming from behind the boulder!" Jonnie slid back down.

Becca's eyes lit up. "That means—"

CJ added, "There really is another room—"

Sierra finished the sentence. "Behind this boulder!"

Jonnie just grinned.

Then she looked puzzled.

"But how are we going to move it to find out what's behind there? It must weigh a ton!" she cried.

Becca checked her glow-in-the-dark watch. "And it's almost time to head back to camp."

The girls' shoulders slumped as they realized they weren't going to have time to even try to move the boulder, let alone see if there was a hidden room. After lunch Susan was going to teach them some new knots and then lead them on a hike, and the day would be over. In the morning, they'd be leaving for home. This was their last chance to explore the caves, their last chance to find Black Bart's gold.

"Come on," Becca said. "We'd better head back, or they'll be sending a search party for us. And then we'll really be the laughingstocks of camp."

But as she followed Sierra out of the caves and back toward camp, Becca couldn't stop thinking about their discovery and the legend of Black Bart's gold.

She was certain it was behind that boulder.

Chapter 11

"Hangtown Fry? What's that?" CJ asked. Susan had just announced what they'd be eating for dinner.

"It was a favorite meal of the old prospectors back in 1849. According to legend, when anyone struck it rich, they ordered a dish made with the three most expensive items at the local café: eggs, bacon, and oysters."

"*Blech!*" CJ made a face and stuck out her tongue. "Gross! I hate oysters."

"Have you ever eaten an oyster, CJ?" Susan asked.

"Uh...not exactly. But I saw one once, and it looked disgusting."

"Well, we're having our last meal at the Nugget Café, and I want you all to taste Hangtown Fry. Then you can have your cheeseburgers, if you must."

"We're going into town again?" Becca spoke up, her eyes wide.

"Yes," Susan said. "I thought it would be fun to eat at the local café in Flat Skunk."

Becca pulled her three friends aside. "This is great! While we're in town, we can borrow a shovel from those old prospectors at the museum and use it to move that rock."

Sierra, Jonnie, and CJ stared at Becca in amazement.

"You don't mean—" Sierra began.

"You're going back—" Jonnie continued.

"Into the caves!" CJ completed the sentence.

Becca nodded. "Why not?"

"Why not?" Sierra repeated, exasperated. "Because we're leaving tomorrow!" Sierra always tried to play by the rules.

Becca nodded. "We still have tonight."

"You're not serious!" Jonnie screeched.

"In the middle of the night?" CJ looked terrified. "You're nuts!"

Becca frowned. "Look, it's our last chance to find the gold. I know it's in Black *Bat* Cave. The entrance to the cave is blocked by that boulder. When we move it—"

"*If* we can move it!" corrected Jonnie. "That thing is huge!"

"Yeah, well, while you guys were washing up for dinner, I thought up a plan." Becca stuck out her pinkie. Sierra, Jonnie, and CJ looked at one another, nodded, and hooked on.

"Okay," said Becca, checking around to see if anyone— Tiffany, in particular—was spying on them. "We'll need a shovel and a board. I'll bet Winky and those old prospectors would lend us a shovel, and I saw some boards lying near the caves' entrance."

"What exactly are we going to do?" CJ asked.

"First, eat fast so we can go over to the museum and talk to Winky."

"Then what?" Jonnie asked.

"Then, after we get back to camp, we'll pretend to go to sleep. Only we'll sneak out and go back to the caves with our flashlights and have another look around."

Susan called them together again, and they headed down the path to the town, singing as they walked. Soon they were enjoying their cheeseburgers and milk shakes at the Nugget Café. The platter of Hangtown Fry that Susan had ordered sat untouched in the middle of the table like a quivering gray centerpiece.

"I wish you girls had just tried it. It's not that bad," Susan said, sipping her coffee.

"I did," Jonnie said, raising her hand.

"How did you like it?"

"The bacon and eggs tasted all right. But the oyster tasted like...rubber. Yuck."

Susan laughed. When the four friends finished eating, she gave them permission to visit the Nugget Museum again.

Becca, Sierra, Jonnie, and CJ found Winky, Sluice, and Panner playing cards in the back room. Sluice's teeth floated in a glass of water sitting on the table next to a wad of cash.

"Hey, scouts!" Winky stood up, grinning. "Welcome back. Want another look around, do ya?"

"Actually," Becca glanced back at her friends for reassurance, "we were wondering if we could borrow a shovel—just for tonight."

Winky's grin faded. "A shovel? What for?"

Becca checked her friends again. They nodded encouragingly. "We...wanted to dig a trap for that mountain lion that's supposed to be around here. Just to be safe, you know."

The old prospectors looked at one another and frowned.

"Well, I guess I have a stubby old camp shovel I could let you borrow," Winky said. "Say, didja ever find that gold you were lookin' for?"

The girls froze.

"Uh...no, of course not," Becca stammered. "It...was just a legend, remember? You said so yourself." The girls forced smiles and tried to look relaxed.

Winky stared at her for a few seconds until Becca finally turned away and pretended to examine one of the museum's geodes.

"Be right back," Winky said finally. As the girls walked slowly around the small museum, Becca felt the eyes of the other two prospectors on her. "Wouldn't want to be caught in a dark cave with them," she thought. "They're funny but weird."

Winky returned with the shovel, and the girls thanked him profusely.

"No need to return it. It's about wore out anyway," Winky said.

Susan arrived moments later, and the girls were relieved to leave.

"What's in your backpack?" Susan asked Jonnie, noticing her lumpy bag.

"Uh...rocks. Sierra found some neat ones outside the museum, and the men said we can keep them as souvenirs."

Susan nodded, seemingly satisfied. Jonnie raised her eyebrows at Becca when Susan looked away, but Becca gave her a thumbs up.

When they got back to camp, the girls headed for their tents to prepare for bed.

"We have to wait at least a half-hour after lights out to make sure it's safe to go," said Becca.

The girls pulled on their pajamas over their clothes and

hopped into their sleeping bags. When Susan arrived for bed check, the other three girls faked sleeping while Becca pretended to read.

"Good-night, Becca," Susan said softly.

"Good-night, Susan. We had a great time. Thanks for taking us here."

Susan smiled, then ducked out of the tent and zipped up the door.

The girls waited until the camp was silent, then waited another thirty minutes.

"Time to go." Becca lightly shook the dozing CJ.

CJ groaned, and Becca quickly slapped a hand over CJ's mouth. CJ's eyes opened wide. Becca shushed her.

Quietly, they peeled off their pajamas, then snatched the shovel, their sweatshirts, flashlights, and fanny packs. After unzipping the door, they tiptoed out of camp toward the caves.

They were off in the middle of the night. Alone.

Not for a second did Becca think what they were doing was really stupid.

Chapter 12

"What was that?" CJ stopped in her tracks.

The girls had almost reached the caves.

"What was what?" Sierra asked.

"I swear I saw something over there."

"Are you sure, CJ?" Jonnie said, pointing her flashlight at some bushes.

"I'm positive," she insisted.

Becca had an awful thought. "What if it's Tiffany and her friends? What if they found out about our plan?" she whispered.

Jonnie crept toward the bushes. "Well, let's find out," she said. She parted the branches and crawled through. The other three watched the beam from her flashlight dart from side to side.

"Whatever was here is gone now," she called. "Let's get going before it's too—Whoa!"

"Jonnie!" the girls cried, rushing toward the bushes.

"I'm okay!" Jonnie assured them. "But I almost fell into a hole."

Becca crawled through the branches. "A hole? Where?" she asked.

"There," Jonnie answered, shining her flashlight on a large pile of leaves.

Becca squatted to get a better look, then immediately stood

and looked around her.

"I know what this is," she announced. "This is Troop 10's trap. They must have forgotten about filling it in after Mrs. Stumplemeyer's...accident."

CJ and Sierra laughed from the other side of the bushes.

"We'll have to let someone know about it tomorrow," Becca said as she and Jonnie crawled back through the bushes to their friends. "I wouldn't want an animal to...." Her voice trailed off while her body stiffened.

The other three turned to her, puzzled.

"What if CJ saw the mountain lion?" she whispered frantically.

The girls stared at one another for a moment before sprinting up the road toward the caves.

"What was *that?*" CJ squeaked.

The girls had just entered the Haunted Caves when they'd heard a low moan echoing through the tunnels.

"Probably nothing," said Sierra, shining her flashlight around the cave walls. "Just the wind."

Becca didn't believe her, but she pushed on, dragging a board she'd found near the entrance. At first the girls moved slowly by the light of their flashlights, but they picked up speed as they neared Black Bat Cave. Becca tried not to listen for noises, but she couldn't help herself. The caves were filled with strange echoes.

Just as they entered Black Bat Cave, the girls heard another moan.

"I heard it again!" said CJ, eyes wide in the glow of her

flashlight. "That moaning! Didn't you hear it?"

The other girls said nothing, but it was clear by their dropped jaws that they had.

Becca shook off her fear. "Come on. Sierra's right. It's just the wind. Let's hurry up before we're missed at camp. CJ, bring the shovel over here."

Becca dropped the board and began sizing up the distance between the boulder and the opposite wall.

"What are you going to do?" CJ asked, handing Becca the shovel.

Becca rested her arm on the handle. "First I'm going to figure out where I can wedge this board between the boulder and the opposite wall. Then we're going to dig a hole under the front of this rock. The board should hold the boulder in place, and when we yank the board away, the boulder should roll into the hole we've dug. That should give us enough room to crawl behind it and find out if there's another cave back there."

"Cool," said Sierra.

Jonnie helped Becca find a good place to wedge the board. Then the girls took turns digging the hole until Becca thought it was wide enough.

"Ready to rock-and-roll?" Becca asked.

The other girls nodded, then all four grabbed hold of the board and yanked it out of place. The huge rock slowly rolled a fraction, then toppled into the hole.

"We did it!" Becca shouted. She flexed her biceps.

"Oh no!" Jonnie moaned. Becca whipped around.

Behind the boulder was a wall.

"I thought you said there'd be a hole behind this rock, Jonnie!" Becca cried.

"I said I felt air coming in. Up at the top. That's all."

"Now you tell me!" Becca wailed. In frustration, she whacked the wall behind the rock with the shovel...and heard a distinctly hollow sound.

The girls looked at one another.

Sierra began knocking the wall. "This wall is fake!"

Becca peered closely at it with her flashlight. "Wow. It's probably made from the stuff they use at Disneyland: Looks real, but I'll bet it's only plastic or something." Becca took another whack at it. A small crack appeared in the middle.

"You're breaking it!" yelled CJ. "Hit it again!"

Becca did, the sound reverberating throughout the cave and echoing down the tunnels. Finally, she broke through.

"You did it! There's another room back there, just like we thought!" Jonnie squatted and poked her hand through the small hole. "Brrr! It's even colder in there!"

Becca whacked the wall a few more times, then dropped the shovel and stuck her shoulders through.

"What do you see?" Sierra asked.

"Nothing. It's pitch black. Give me my flashlight."

Sierra handed it over. Becca turned it on and peered inside.

"I...I see something...shiny...in the corner!" Becca squealed.

The girls pressed against her, trying to see inside. Becca pulled back to let each one see for herself.

With renewed energy, the girls took turns whacking at the wall to make the hole larger.

When it seemed big enough, CJ said decidedly, "I'm going to try to squeeze through." After some squirming, grunting, and wiggling, she reached the other side. "Wow!" she said, gazing at the geodes shimmering in her flashlight beam.

"She did it!" said Sierra. "I'm going next!"

One by one the girls wiggled into the dark, cold room. Then all four shined their flashlights at the far corner and moved closer toward the shiny spot.

"It's a box!" CJ said. A large wooden box, crisscrossed with gold metal strips.

"It looks more like a treasure chest," Sierra added.

The girls giggled.

"Do you think it's Black Bart's hidden gold?" Jonnie asked.

"Let's find out," said Becca, as she neared the box.

The wooden box was secured with a rusty lock. Becca tugged at it, but it didn't give. "Wait here," she said, ducking back through the hole. She returned seconds later with the shovel. She slowly lifted it above her head, then slammed it down on the lock. It broke open.

"You did it!" CJ squealed. She took a deep breath and forced open the lid. The others crowded around her.

"Oh...my...gosh!" said CJ. Gold jewelry, gold coins, and gold nuggets glittered up at the girls.

Before CJ could reach for the pocket watch on top, they heard a moan.

All four girls froze.

"Wait a minute!" Becca whispered. "That was no moaning ghost. I know exactly what that is!" She yelled toward the opening,

"Tiffany! Knock it off! It's not funny anymore! We found the treasure and you didn't, so just quit—"

The moaning turned to deep, thunderous laughter.

"Tiffany?" CJ squeaked.

Something moved on the other side of the hole. The girls shined their flashlights at it, the beams shaking.

Suddenly, a huge head wearing a ski mask appeared in the light.

The girls' screams rang through the cave.

No one—except the intruder—heard them.

Chapter 13

"Shuuuut uuuup!" the masked stranger bellowed.

Definitely not Tiffany. Scouts aren't supposed to say "shut up." Besides, this voice was unmistakably male.

Becca scanned the cave for the shovel. At least she might be able to defend them with it.

"Shoot," she whispered. After she'd broken the lock, Becca had flung the shovel aside. It now lay near the hole.

And it was too late for her to run and grab it. The giant masked man was now inside the cave. He snatched the shovel and towered over them.

"One man with a shovel," Becca thought. "I bet the four of us could still take him." She started to think of ways to distract him, but before she could put a plan into action, another masked head popped through the hole.

There were two of them.

Becca glanced at her friends. Jonnie and Sierra tried to stifle their screams. CJ's eyes widened, her fists clenched tightly.

"What do you want?" Becca forced herself to take charge. "Our troop leader is on her way, and if—"

"Shut up!" snarled the second stranger. His voice was scratchy and hoarse. And he mumbled as if he had marbles in his mouth.

Becca took a step back. She was frightened, but more than that, she was angry.

How had these men found them? Had they been following them the whole time? And did they know about the treasure the girls had worked so hard to find?

"Move aside," the bigger one commanded. "Lemme see what you got there."

The girls huddled around the treasure, but the smaller man pulled out a large hunting knife and waved it at them. The scouts backed off. His partner squatted and stared at the opened box, speechless.

Becca could almost see the sparkling loot reflected in his eyes.

"Holy cow!" he shouted.

"We're rich!" his buddy crowed.

The four girls looked at one another.

"That's ours!" Becca said bravely. "We found it, and we're turning it over to the museum."

The two masked men burst out laughing. The one with the knife took a menacing step toward them, while the other tried to pick up the box of loot.

"It's too heavy," he gasped.

"We'll drag it," said his partner. They each grabbed a handle with one hand and pulled it toward the opening, the knife and the shovel clasped in their other hands. Becca watched for an opportunity to do something—anything—but the men kept an eye on them the whole time.

"I'll go through the hole first, then you push the box through," the smaller man mumbled to his buddy. "Make sure you watch them girls." He handed him the knife.

The giant man nodded and glared at them. His partner wiggled through the opening, then reached back in and took hold of the box. After a couple of minutes, they managed to get the gold-filled box to the other side.

While the two men were distracted, Becca caught a glimpse of Jonnie's fingers moving rapidly at her side.

She was fingerspelling something!

"F-L-A-S-H-L-I-G-H-T"

Becca nodded, then slowly pulled her flashlight behind her, flicking off the light. The other girls did the same. The big man didn't notice the sudden darkness and started to crawl out the hole feet first. The girls waited, their flashlights ready for action. Becca's heart beat double time.

"Now!" Becca yelled when he was halfway through the hole. The four girls rushed forward and began battering him with their flashlights.

"Hey, cut it out!" he squawked, raising his arms to defend himself. The girls continued to strike him. But instead of fleeing the cave as Becca had hoped, the man charged back inside.

He pulled out the knife and flashed it at the stunned foursome.

"I said, CUT IT OUT!" He jabbed at the air in front of CJ. She jumped backward, tripped, and fell down. "Gimme them flashlights!" No one moved. "NOW!"

The girls surrendered their weapons to the man, who threw them one by one through the hole to his partner. "Hiding anything else I'm gonna want?" he asked.

The girls shook their heads. Becca thought about her first-aid pack, but she kept still and willed herself not to give anything else away.

"Now don't move, or I'll come back and take those pretty earrings you girls are wearin'. The *hard* way." He twisted the knife in the air as if he were gutting a chicken. CJ gasped.

Still pointing the knife at them, the masked man backed out of the opening and disappeared.

The girls took a collective deep breath. "They're gone!" whispered Jonnie. CJ got to her feet and brushed herself off. Becca listened hard to make sure the two men were really gone.

Suddenly the girls heard a scraping sound, then some heavy grunting and a little cursing.

They looked at the hole.

In seconds, it was no longer there. The two men had rolled the boulder back, blocking their way out.

The room went pitch black.

Chapter 14

"They've blocked the hole with the boulder!" CJ squealed. "We're trapped!"

"We'll get out of here somehow, CJ," Becca said, her mouth dry with fear. "Don't worry. I'll figure out something. After all, I'm the one who got us into this mess." The girls groped in the dark for one another, then grasped hands.

One of the girls sniffled. "They're as scared as I am," Becca realized. "We've got to keep level heads." The cave was chilly, and she was thankful for the sweatshirt she'd brought. She only wished they had a fire...

That was it! Becca reached behind her and unzipped her fanny pack. Carefully, she felt inside the first-aid kit and found a book of matches. She struck one, and the cave dimly lit up.

CJ shrieked.

"What?" Becca jumped. "CJ! You almost made me drop the match."

"I stepped in something! Soft...and gooshy... like slime..."

Becca squatted and saw the imprint of CJ's shoe.

"Yuck!" CJ said, appalled. "What is it?"

Sierra knelt. "Bat guano," she said.

"What's guano?"

"Doo-doo."

CJ looked even more horrified. "Oh gross! I'm going to be sick!"

"No, you're not." Becca felt the flame begin to heat her fingertips. The light would only last a few more seconds. "Listen, we only have four matches left. We're going to have to use them carefully. First, let's see if there's any chance we can push that boulder out of the way."

The first match went out.

"Oh great!" muttered Jonnie. "Now we're down to three."

Becca lit another match, and the girls dashed to the hole and began pushing the huge rock. It didn't budge. After the match burned out, Becca heard her friends sigh, defeated.

"Okay," she consented. "It's too big to move from this side."

"We're trapped," CJ repeated.

"And no one knows we're here," Jonnie added.

"I know, I know, but I'm sure—" Becca felt something whiz by her head.

"CJ? Was that you?" Becca whispered.

"Was what me?"

"Did you...move your arm by my head just a second ago?"

"No. I haven't moved from this spot."

"Sierra? Jonnie?"

Before they could answer, Becca gasped. "There it was again! Who did that?"

She scrambled to light another match, and then she held it high.

"Bats!" Jonnie screeched. "This cave is full of bats!"

CJ ducked while the others watched the ceiling come alive with fluttering wings and swooping bodies.

"They won't attack," Sierra said, fascinated.

"She loves this kind of stuff," Becca thought. "Thank goodness she's here."

"But one of them brushed by my head," Jonnie said.

"It wasn't after you. It was probably just trying to get out. Bats are nocturnal, you know."

"What's *nocturnal* mean?" CJ whispered.

"They sleep during the day and fly at night. This really must be the Black Bat Cave! Cool!"

Just then, the third match burned out. The girls froze, listening to the racket of the bats' wings as they fled the cave.

"They won't hurt you," Sierra said.

"But it's dark in here. They'll crash into us just flying around," Becca said.

"No they won't. They use radar to keep from flying into things."

"What about sucking our blood?" Jonnie asked. "I saw this movie once—"

"That's not true either," Sierra said. "They eat insects, not human blood. They only want out of here. Almost as bad as we do."

Becca sucked in her breath. "But they *are* getting out of here! That means there's a way out!"

The girls listened to the frenzied flying for a few more minutes. Suddenly the cave was quiet again. The cold began seeping through Becca's sweatshirt. She shivered.

"Where did they go?" CJ asked.

"That's what I plan to find out," Becca said. She lit the second-to-last match just in time to see a few final bats fly through a crack of faint light about ten feet up the wall.

"Up there!" Sierra pointed. The girls stared where the bats had disappeared. Becca was sure she saw some stalagmites jutting from a ledge and thought she saw a shadow, as if there might be a small cave up there. And maybe an opening to the outside, too?

"This match is about to burn out, and I only have one left, so listen carefully," Becca said. "Take off your shirts, but leave your sweatshirts on. We'll tie them together, and I'll tie one end to this broken stalagmite using a larkshead knot, like Susan taught us today."

Sierra and Jonnie nodded. CJ looked skeptical.

Becca continued, "When I light the last match, Jonnie, you throw it toward those stalagmites up on that ledge. If we can snag it between two of them, we can climb up and see if there's some kind of exit."

The flame burned Becca's fingers. "Ouch!" She dropped the match, and it went out as it fell to the ground.

One match left.

"Okay, scouts, let's go."

Working only by touch, they soon made what felt to be a ten-foot-long T-shirt rope. Becca measured the length by stretching the rope from her chest to the tips of her fingers.

"Time to light the last match. Jonnie, are you ready to throw the rope?" Becca handed Jonnie the end with the stalag-mite tied to it.

"I hope I can do it!" Jonnie's voice quavered in the darkness.

"You can." Becca encouraged her. "You pitch no-hitters in

softball all the time. You can do this. Ready, everyone?"

Three yeses echoed in the cave.

The chilly air was beginning to get to Becca. She lit the last match.

"Go for it, Jonnie!"

Jonnie looked as if she was estimating the distance. She took a deep breath, leaned to one side with the rope looped in her hand, then tossed it up.

"Missed!" she said disgustedly, as the rope dropped beside her.

"It's okay," Becca said, checking the match. They only had a few more seconds before the light would burn out—forever. "Relax. Just try again."

Jonnie took another deep breath, then tossed up the rope again. This time she managed to catch it between two stalagmites but not securely enough. The rope fell back down.

"Darn it!" Jonnie sounded desperate. "I can't do it!"

"Yes, you can," Becca said forcefully. She looked at the match. The flame had almost reached her fingers. "Try once more."

Jonnie pinched her lips, focused, and took her stance. Once more she sucked in a deep breath, leaned back, then flung the rope.

And then the room went pitch black.

Chapter 15

"Oh no!" CJ squealed.

Becca was sure the next thing she'd hear would be the rope thumping to the ground. Instead, she heard something else: a clink. High up.

"What was that?"

"I...think I got it!" Jonnie said excitedly.

Becca groped to find Jonnie, then felt Jonnie's arm tighten as she yanked on the rope.

"You hooked it?" Becca felt Jonnie give another yank. "Will it hold?"

"I think so. Feels pretty solid. I'm going to give it a try anyway."

"No," Becca said suddenly.

"What do you mean 'no'?" Jonnie asked.

"I mean, I'm going to climb up first. I'm the one who got us into this, and I'm the one who's going to get us out."

"But you've never done anything like this, Becca," Jonnie protested.

"I've climbed up trees before. It's only about ten feet or so. Besides, I'm the thinnest. I'll be the lightest on the rope. I can do this."

"I think," she said to herself.

"At least I'm going to try," she said aloud.

"Becca, you're crazy," Sierra's voice came from behind her.

Becca turned to face her. "I know. So what else is new? But I'm still going to do this. Jonnie, hand me the end of the rope, please."

The rope slapped against her palm. She first gave it a gentle tug, then a more forceful one, seeing if it would really hold her weight.

"Okay, I'm heading up." Becca took a deep breath, then felt her way to the wall to begin her climb. She felt a stalagmite about a foot up from the ground, stepped against it, and pulled herself up.

"Keep talking, Becca," CJ said. "We can't see how you're doing."

"You'll hear me if I don't make it." Becca forced a small laugh. "Watch out below. Just be sure to keep the rope taut from the bottom."

She heard the girls take a few steps back. "I guess they thought I was serious about falling," she thought. She felt another stalagmite with her foot and continued her slow climb up the rocky surface. Being a little over five feet tall herself, Becca figured she only had about five feet to climb before she'd reach the ledge and the opening she hoped was there. She'd soon know.

"How's it going?" Sierra called after a few minutes. "Sounds like you're getting pretty high up."

Becca had trouble answering. It took all her concentration just to climb. Finding footholds wasn't easy, and the rope felt as if it might give at any moment. The T-shirts had stretched, and

Becca could hear the makeshift grappling hook scraping just above her. But she couldn't see anything. She had no idea how secure that hook really was. Or how long it would last.

"Okay," she finally gasped. "I think I'm almost at the top...I can feel some cold air blowing in."

The girls called out encouragingly, but Becca barely heard them. Her mind kept repeating, "You can do this," while her hands and feet continued to find footholds.

Suddenly Becca heard a rip.

The rope! It was starting to tear. She gasped.

"Are you all right?" Jonnie called up.

Becca couldn't speak. All she could manage were a few grunts. Then she cried, "Oh...my gosh!"

"What? What is it?"

Just as she touched the edge of the ledge, she heard the rope rip again. This time the girls below heard it, too.

"What was that?" CJ demanded.

Becca said nothing. She had to find something to hold onto to. Reaching upward, she brushed against one of the stalagmites anchoring the rope. She grabbed hold of it and tried to climb onto the ledge. She felt a searing pain as her leg slammed against the sharp edge. Straightening her arms, she dragged the other leg up and hoisted herself onto the ledge.

Panting, she looked down into blackness.

"I...made it!" she finally gasped.

"She made it! She made it!" the girls whooped.

And then they all heard something hit the ground.

"Uh-oh," Becca called out. She heard the girls gasp. "What

happened?"

"It's the rope," Jonnie called back. "And our grappling hook."

Becca felt around her. The stalagmite she'd grabbed onto was lying on its side. She shuddered. If it had broken off only a few seconds earlier, she'd be lying on the ground with that rope. She didn't want to think about the road-kill she would have resembled if that had happened.

But now she had a different problem. With the rope on the ground—and nothing to anchor it—the other three wouldn't be able to climb up.

Becca quickly assessed the situation. "Listen, there's a big flat surface up here, just like we thought," she called down. "It's another cave, I'm sure of it. And guess what?"

"What? What?"

"It's covered in bat guano!"

"Eeeeeuuuwwwww!"

"And that's not all."

"What else?"

"There's a tiny little bit of light! I think it's moonlight!"

A cheer rose up through the chilly air.

"There's a hole just above me where the bats must fly out," Becca continued. "It...seems to be covered with branches or something, and it's not very big, but I think I can squeeze though. Hold on..."

Silence. The girls waited anxiously as Becca broke off branches and threw them aside. Soon she'd uncovered the opening, and she crawled through the hole and into the beautiful moonlit night.

Chapter 16

Becca stood up and gazed at her surroundings. This was a heavily wooded part of the park. No wonder no one had ever found this opening. It was practically buried in brambles.

Her arms were stinging, and she held them up to examine them. Even through her sweatshirt, thorns had managed to scrape and stab her flesh. She was bleeding from several places. As she tried to rub the pain away, she heard the other three calling her name.

"Bec-caaaaa!"

"I'm out! I'm free!" she yelled into the hole. "I'm going for help! I'll get Susan and some of the rangers, and we'll be back right away to get you out! Hold tight!"

She heard a muffled cheer and smiled...through tears.

Ignoring the cuts on her legs and arms, Becca found the Big Dipper in the sky and then the North Star. She knew the caves were south of camp, so if she followed the North Star, she was sure to find the road back to Camp Miwok. She raced forward, dodging rocks and branches.

Becca soon stumbled upon the road just before the entrance to the caves and broke into a full run. She'd sprinted just a hundred feet when she saw light from a flashlight heading straight toward her.

Could it be one of the masked men?

A shiver ran up Becca's spine as she ducked behind a bush. She wasn't taking any chances.

As the figure approached, Becca crouched lower, trying not to make any noise. She heard a twig break beneath her foot—and froze. The figure, nearly upon her, stopped. The light whirled toward Becca's bush.

"Who's there?" a voice called out.

"Susan!" Becca yelled, jumping up. "Oh, Susan! I'm so glad to see you!" She ran out and hugged her troop leader, tears streaming down her face.

"Rebecca Matthews!" Susan said sharply. "What are you doing here? I've been frantic! Where are Sierra and Jonnie and CJ?"

Becca tried to tell Susan the whole story. It came out in a jumble, but Susan quickly got the gist of it.

Susan took hold of Becca's arm. "Where are they now?"

Becca pointed to the cave. "I'll show you. But I think we need help to get them out. Maybe we should call a ranger or—"

Just then, they heard an engine and saw headlights appear from around the bend in the road. A truck stopped in front of them. Susan and Becca tried to make out who was driving. "This could be the help we need," thought Becca, straining to see through the glare of the headlights.

The driver rolled down the window and craned his head outside. "Howdy, ladies! Out kinda late, aren't you?"

"Winky!" Becca exclaimed.

"Mr. Pike!" said Susan, relieved. "Thank goodness you're

out here, too. Becca's friends are trapped in the Haunted Caves. We need to get them out. Can you help?"

"Course I can! I been over at the museum cleaning up. Got picks and shovels and ropes and all kinds of stuff with me all the time. Never know when you might strike gold. Hop in and tell me what happened."

As they drove the short distance back to the cave entrance, Becca retold her story, doing a better job of it this time since she could think more clearly. Winky bobbed his head, attentive the whole time.

"That's how I managed to get out," Becca concluded as they climbed out of the truck. "If we can move the rock or get a rope down through the bat opening, we can get them out."

Winky pulled out a pocket watch. He shined his flashlight on it, and it sparkled in the light. "It's two in the mornin'. Sheriff should be home by now. I'll give him a call for backup." He pulled out his cell phone and dialed. "A modern miner," Becca thought. And then she froze.

She looked at Winky's wrist as he muttered into the phone. It was bare.

The watch!

Winky had been wearing a wristwatch when she had seen him at the museum that night—the one he said he'd found in the caves, left by a tourist. That watch was gone, and Winky now had a very expensive gold pocket watch—the old-fashioned kind that her great-grandfather used to carry.

Just like the watch she'd seen lying on top of Black Bart's treasure when CJ had opened the box.

Winky!

It must have been *his* men who robbed them and left them sealed up inside the cave! The mumbler and the giant with the big head were Sluice and Panner!

Winky glanced at Becca. "It's gonna be okay, honey," he assured her. "The sheriff's on his way. Now let's go see if we can find your friends." He returned to his phone call.

The sheriff wasn't on his way. Becca was sure Winky wasn't talking to him. "But I'll bet he's talking to his two buddies," she thought.

At that instant, Becca knew she and Susan were in big trouble. Winky clicked off the phone and hooked it onto his belt.

Becca turned to Susan and gave her a hand signal she'd learned last year when the troop had visited a Native American reservation.

"Danger," she signed, thrusting her fist downward, while Winky walked ahead of them toward the cave. "Trap!" Becca clasped her two hands together.

Susan looked puzzled. Becca repeated both signs. Susan nodded tentatively, still frowning. Becca knew she had to act fast if she was going to save her friends, her troop leader, and herself.

"If only we could distract Winky somehow and get his cell phone," she thought, staring down the road.

When Becca saw the nearby clearing bathed in moonlight, she snapped to attention. "That's it!" She had a plan, but she'd better act fast before Sluice and Panner arrived.

She screamed at the top of her lungs.

Winky whirled around. "What is it? What's wrong?"

Becca pointed into the dark forest. "There! I saw something!"

Winky squinted and shined his flashlight into the trees. She knew he guessed it couldn't be his men already. It would take them a few more minutes to arrive.

She screamed again. "There! Oh my gosh! A mountain lion! I see it!" She pointed again, looking horror-stricken. "There! There!"

Winky stuffed one hand under his belt and pulled out something.

Susan and Becca looked at each other in terror.

Winky had a gun.

Chapter 17

For a moment, Becca thought the gun was aimed at them. Then she realized Winky was pointing it toward the trees.

"There!" she said quickly, pulling herself together. "Over there by that tree!"

Winky started walking warily toward the forest.

Susan started to say something, but Becca motioned her to keep quiet. Becca caught up with Winky, frantically gesturing for him to follow her toward the clearing. "I'm sure it was a mountain lion. I thought I saw it around here earlier today. And now I'm sure of it!"

Winky squinted some more. He started to lower the gun. "I don't see nothin'—"

"There!" It was Susan! She may not have known exactly what Becca was up to, but she trusted her scout enough to believe Winky wasn't to be trusted. "I see it! In those bushes!"

Becca slyly grinned at her, then focused on the fictional mountain lion. Winky raised his gun again and swung his flashlight from side to side.

"Oh gosh, there it goes! Over there!" Becca cried.

"I see it, Mr. Pike! Do something!" Susan pleaded.

They winked at each other in the pale moonlight.

Winky was too busy watching for some sign of the mountain lion to notice the wink. Slowly he stepped farther into the bushes.

Becca and Susan followed close behind, encouraging him with every step.

"He's right over there!" Becca pointed to a line of trees beyond the bushes.

"I still don't see nothin'—" Winky said, starting to turn back.

Becca didn't hesitate. It was now or never. She rushed at him with all her strength and knocked him off balance.

"What the—" Winky never finished his sentence. He disappeared into Troop 10's animal trap. His gun lay next to the hole where he'd dropped it as he fell.

"Becca!" Susan gasped. "How did you know that trap was still there?" She carefully grabbed the gun by the handle and turned to Winky. "Mr. Pike," she said, "I suggest you toss me that cell phone."

Winky grudgingly did so, and Becca caught the phone. She dialed 911 and explained the situation to the dispatcher.

"The sheriff's on his way, Susan," she said, clicking off the phone.

Becca heard Winky cursing and peered into the hole. He was lying on his side and clutching his ankle, which was bent at an odd angle.

"Come on," she said to Susan. "I have to tell the girls that help is coming. I'm sure they're scared and wondering if I'm ever coming back."

Susan smiled at Becca. "They know you're coming back, Becca. You don't have to worry about that. Now wipe that grin off your face, scout," she barked. "You're in deep doo-doo, don't forget. When this is all over, we're going to have a talk."

Becca nodded sheepishly, then led the way to the bat opening.

"Jonnie? CJ? Sierra? Are you all right?" Becca called down the hole.

"Yeah, Becca," Jonnie's voice echoed up. "Cold, hungry, a little scared, but we're fine. Did you get help?"

"Yep, the sheriff is on his way. And Susan is here."

Silence. Becca looked at Susan.

"Hi, girls. Are you okay down there?" Susan called gently.

"Hi, Susan! We're so sorry!" came all three voices.

"Don't worry about that now. I'm just glad you're safe. You owe a lot to Becca for your rescue. She's got quite a story to tell."

"Yeah, we owe her big time," called CJ. "For getting us into this mess!" Becca could hear the girls giggling. Thank goodness they weren't really that mad at her.

Susan and Becca told the girls they were going to meet the sheriff at the caves' entrance, and the two quickly tramped back through the brambles.

Moments later Becca heard several cars driving up the road.

"I'm Sheriff Mercer," the uniformed man said, stepping out of his patrol car at the caves' entrance. "What's going on here? My dispatcher said you got some scouts stuck in the caves."

Becca explained what had happened. When she told them about Winky and his cohorts, the sheriff raised an eyebrow.

"I knew he was up to something, but I could never catch him," he said. "The only reason he ran the museum was so he could get first crack at anything of value. When we get that treasure box back, it'll be turned over to the county museum. Under the supervision of a new curator, of course."

"But what if they're gone? What if they've already left with the gold and stuff?" Becca suddenly realized.

"Not much chance of that. I got a call about two men disturbing the peace downtown. Sounds like they're celebrating. They should be drunk as skunks by now. Easy pickings for us."

Becca cleared her throat. "Speaking of skunks…"

Susan took over. "You might want to check one of our troops' animal traps, Sheriff. You'll find the ringleader there." She pointed toward the pit.

Becca grinned.

The sheriff nodded at his deputy to take care of it. "He was probably on his way to get the rest of the treasure. Now here's what we're gonna do," he explained. "These officers will go into the cave and see if they can move that rock that's blocking the entrance. I'll bring some rope from the patrol car. One way or the other we'll get them outta there."

Susan led the sheriff to the bat opening, while Becca led the officers to Black Bat Cave. As they drew nearer to the entrance, they heard singing:

The worms crawl in,
The worms crawl out…

Becca knew then her friends were definitely going to be all right.

Within ten minutes, the officers managed to roll back the boulder, and the girls scrambled out to freedom.

After Susan hugged the scouts until she was convinced they were okay, they all rode back to camp in the sheriff's patrol car. Thank goodness he didn't use the lights or sirens.

"Might wake the other campers," he'd said.

"All I need is for Tiffany to find out about this, and we'd never hear the end of it," thought Becca.

Back at Camp Miwok, the girls thanked the sheriff for his help.

"You know, you scouts could have been in real trouble back there," he scolded. "If the place had caved in, or there really was a mountain lion loose, you might not be here right now."

Then he smiled. "But I have to admit, you found the gold we've been searching for when nobody else could find it. You may get a reward out of this for helping the town museum."

The girls swelled with pride. But then they caught a glimpse of Susan's frown, and their grins faded.

"Thank you, Sheriff Mercer. Good-night." Susan turned to the girls. "You four, go to bed!" She gave each girl another hug. "We'll talk about this in the morning."

The scouts nodded and headed for their tent after a quick stop at the latrine. They slipped into their pajamas and wiggled into their sleeping bags. It took a while for the bags to warm them up, thanks to the chill in the caves. But it wasn't long before CJ, Jonnie, and Sierra were asleep, exhausted from the adventure.

Becca lay awake thinking about all that had happened. Troop 13 had won the Jamboree. Jonnie had received the highest honor, a Leadership Pin. They'd found Black Bart's hidden treasure. They'd been trapped in a bat cave by masked robbers *and* lived to tell about it. They might even get a badge out of it.

It had been a pretty good weekend.

Chapter 18

Early the next day, the scouts from Troop 13 ate breakfast, broke down their campsite, and prepared for the bus ride back to San Francisco. Just as the four friends finished loading their gear onto the bus, Tiffany and her pals appeared.

"We just wanted to say good-bye," Tiffany said, smiling. Becca couldn't tell if the smile was real or fake. "It was fun competing against you. Sorry about the underpants thing. **And** tying your clothes into knots. And trying to scare you in the cave."

Becca shrugged. "That's okay. It was kinda fun. Sorry about trapping you in your tent. And psyching you out in the cave. And the wet sleeping bags."

Tiffany blinked and glanced at the other girls. "What wet sleeping bags?"

Becca flushed. Her friends coughed and looked away. "I...uh, I meant—"

"You poured *water* in our sleeping bags last night? I thought I had wet my pants!" Tiffany screamed.

"Me, too!" cried her three friends.

Then they began to laugh. "Good one," said Tiffany. "Well, we'll get you back next year."

"Yeah, right," said Becca.

"Here." Tiffany held out a small box to Becca. "We made

you a going-away present. You can open it on the bus if you want."

Becca was surprised at the gesture. "Thanks, Tiffany, Stephanie, Gina, Joanne, everyone. That's really sweet of you. We didn't get you anything." She felt bad. Maybe they weren't so awful after all.

"That's okay. We just wanted to say no hard feelings. See you next year." With that, Tiffany and her friends turned, flipping their long ponytails, and headed for their bus back to Sacramento.

"All aboard!" shouted Susan, clipboard in hand. She counted the girls as they stepped onto the bus. "Thank goodness," Becca heard her whisper. Was she grateful they were all present or that they were finally leaving camp?

As the girls found their seats, Susan stood at the front of the bus and read her usual list of rules and announcements. Becca pulled out the box Tiffany had given them and untied the twine. She opened the top and peeked in.

Inside was a pile of bat guano.

Becca looked out the window, half-expecting to see Tiffany standing there, laughing at her oh-so-hilarious joke. But her bus had already left.

Becca scanned the manzanita bushes one last time. She thought she saw something swishing its tail in them, but couldn't be sure. By the time she got the others to look, whatever it was had disappeared.

"And one more thing before we go, scouts," Susan said, reclaiming everyone's attention.

"Becca, Jonnie, Sierra, and CJ, a special badge for bravery, perseverance, and ingenuity, awarded by the Calaveras County sheriff."

The four friends' faces lit up.

"Of course," she added, " you'll have to promise you'll never go out alone at night again without my permission."

The girls nodded eagerly.

"And, you'll have cleanup duty for the next three months for not following the scouting rules."

Their smiles turned to pouts, and the rest of the scouts ribbed them good-naturedly.

Susan handed the friends each a Local Legend badge and returned to the front of the bus. "And now, buckle up. We're heading back to San Francisco."

"Susan," Becca called out. "Where are we going on our next field trip?"

Susan gave a curious smile. "I'll give you a hint. You're going someplace to learn how to be equestrians."

Becca grinned. Horseback riding!

She couldn't wait!